CRUNCH!

I twist around.

Standing in the woods no more than forty feet away is the biggest bear I have ever seen, in or out of a glass display. On its hind legs it must be twelve feet at least.

A shiver of ice-cold fear grips me from head to foot. Right now I'm so scared that I can't move.

The bear is up on its hind legs, turning its head, squinting and sniffing. It smells something, but it can't see exactly what.

Thump! I actually feel the ground shake as the bear drops back down to all fours. It starts toward me!

AGAINST THE ODDS™: Shark Bite
AGAINST THE ODDS™: Grizzly Attack

By Todd Strasser

From Minstrel Books
Published by Pocket Books

TODD STRASSER

AGAINST THE ODDS™

GRIZZLY ATTACK

A
MINSTREL®
BOOK

Published by POCKET BOOKS
New York   London   Toronto   Sydney   Tokyo   Singapore

This book is a work of fiction. Names, characters, places and incidents are products of the author's imagination or are used fictitiously. Any resemblance to actual events or locales or persons, living or dead, is entirely coincidental.

A MINSTREL PAPERBACK *Original*

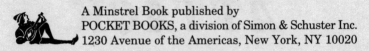 A Minstrel Book published by
POCKET BOOKS, a division of Simon & Schuster Inc.
1230 Avenue of the Americas, New York, NY 10020

™ and Copyright © 1998 by Todd Strasser

ISBN: 0-671-02310-1

First Minstrel Books printing December 1998

10 9 8 7 6 5 4 3 2 1

A MINSTREL BOOK and colophon are registered trademarks of Simon & Schuster Inc.

Front cover illustration by Franco Accornero

Printed in the U.S.A.

To Rebecca and Samantha Gilbert

GRIZZLY
ATTACK

1

Anchorage Airport, Anchorage, Alaska

I'm in the airport in Anchorage, Alaska, staring up at a fifteen-foot-tall totem pole with carved, colorful faces of birds and bears. I've never seen an airport like this. It's half-airport, half-museum. It has check-in and ticket counters like a regular airport. But it also has totem poles and display cases with stuffed animals and kayaks in them.

It's a little confusing for a twelve-year-old kid from San Francisco. The sign says the kayak is made of sealskin. I understand that. But totem poles? I thought Eskimos lived on ice. Where did they get wood for a totem pole?

1

The other thing about this airport is the people. They're not your typical TV commercial types in business suits lugging briefcases. Just about everyone is wearing jeans and plaid lumberjack shirts, cowboy boots, or work shoes. The men have long hair and scraggly beards. The women have long hair and wear boots. There's hardly a skirt or dress in sight. And instead of briefcases they're lugging small outboard motors and giant-size boxes of Pampers.

I move over to the next display case. This one's filled with miniature canoes and seals carved out of whalebone and teeth. According to the plaque, these things are called scrimshaw.

To tell you the truth, this stuff doesn't usually interest me, but I have time to kill. How much time? I don't honestly know. I've been here since yesterday afternoon. Last night—well, the clocks said it was night, but it never actually got dark. It just sort of turned twilight—I slept on a couple of chairs pushed together. I was worried the security guards might kick me out, but I never saw any guards and nobody seemed to care that I was sleeping there. I guess that's one of the advantages of being twelve years old and by yourself.

I'm waiting for someone, but I don't know what he looks like. Just that his name is Duke. Meanwhile, I eat potato chips and Milk Duds and look at the displays. Right now I'm staring up at an old Piper Cub airplane suspended by cables from the ceiling. A sign says the plane used to belong to C. D. Betts, famous Alaskan bush pilot. It says a bush pilot is someone who flies into the wilderness in any kind of weather and lands on anything that looks flat and firm. It says C. D. Betts was a bush pilot for forty-three years and died in his sleep at the age of eighty-six.

I guess he was lucky.

I hope I get lucky and this Duke guy shows up soon.

I know kids who've gone to camp for the summer. But to be twelve years old and come alone all the way to Alaska must be some kind of record. Last night I spoke to my mom on the phone. She sort of freaked out when I told her that my uncle Jake wasn't here to meet me when I arrived. Uncle Jake's her brother, although she hasn't seen him in a long, long time and I've never actually met him.

But then I explained that there was a message waiting for me from Uncle Jake saying he would've come to meet me, but he wasn't feeling well. So he arranged for this guy Duke to come get me. It's kind of weird. Uncle Jake must be the last person on earth who doesn't have a

3

phone. In the meantime, Mom said I should stay at the airport and wait.

Like I've got a lot of other places to go?

I wander over to the counter where the bush pilots book their flights. They must fly a lot of hunters and fishermen around because there are all kinds of stuffed fish on the walls and stuffed animals in glass cases. Wolves, a grizzly bear, a lynx, some wolverines . . . all posed menacingly with their lips drawn up in snarls, revealing long pointed teeth.

It bothers me that they had to kill these animals and stick them behind glass. I guess it's how the bush pilots advertise. But why couldn't they just have pictures of the animals instead of killing them?

Even stuffed and on display, the grizzly is totally scary. Standing on his hind legs he's about eight feet tall with pointed teeth bared and these amazingly long claws. Six inches, at least. The sign says they're razor sharp. I think he could take a swipe at you and you'd be sliced bread. Like Wile E. Coyote in a Road Runner cartoon or something. I'm surprised a Hollywood moviemaker hasn't put one of these bears in a bullet-proof vest and sent it on a rampage through some town: INVASION OF THE INDE-STRUCTIBLE KILLER GRIZZLIES.

"Your name Tyler?" a voice asks.

4

I turn around and see a broad red-and-blue plaid shirt with a torn pocket and brown cloth patches on both elbows. Gazing higher I see a man with squinty blue eyes, a big bushy blond beard, and long dirty blond hair pulled back in a braided ponytail. He's huge, maybe six and a half feet tall. Big enough to be an offensive linesman for the 49ers. I have no doubt he's the biggest person I've ever spoken to in my life.

"Tyler Duvall," I tell him.

"Duke Hodge." The man holds out his hand and we shake. It's like shaking hands with a baseball glove. "You're pretty young to come this far alone, aren't you?"

"My mom says I'm mature for my age," I reply. "You know what city kids are like."

Duke hooks his thumbs in his pockets. "Can't say I do. Never been to Frisco myself. Don't have much interest in going, neither."

I bet Duke wants me to ask him why and then he can tell me all about his life as a wilderness man or whatever, but right now my mind's on other stuff.

"Do you know my uncle?" I ask.

"Jake? Yup. He's up at his cabin on the Kantishna River, asked me to give you a lift."

"Do we go by boat?" I ask.

"Heck, no. We fly," Duke says. "Only civilized

way to get around up here. Now let's get going.
We got some miles to put under our tails."

I get my stuff and meet Duke at the bush
pilots' counter.

"What's that?" He points at the five-foot-long
tube I'm carrying.

"Fly rod."

"That's the kind of fishing you do?"

"No, I just carry it around for fun."

Duke squints at me with those beady blue
eyes. They're probably not that small. It's just
that the rest of him is so large. He grins know-
ingly. "Wise guy, huh?"

"Well, like I said, I come from the big city."

Duke starts to push open a door that says:
AUTHORIZED PERSONNEL ONLY.

"Aren't we missing someone?" I ask, hesi-
tating.

"Like who?" Duke asks.

"Like the pilot or someone?"

Duke's scowl turns into a smile. "Who do you
think I am, the stewardess?"

I guess my jaw drops a little. *He's my pilot?*

"Don't worry." He grins. "I've been flying for
thirty-five years, and I've only crashed four
times."

Uh . . . Am I supposed to feel reassured?

2

We go through a door and out onto the wet runway. It's been nothing but grayness and rain since I arrived yesterday.

I step around the puddles, inhale the damp air, and feel the cold drops of rain hit my face. Above us the sky is slate gray except for the low white puffs of clouds racing past. Duke and I pass dozens of planes lashed to the ground. They came in all shapes, colors, and sizes—from tiny two-seaters to big old transport props with their passenger windows painted over. Duke shields his eyes from the wind-driven rain.

"Nice afternoon," he says.

For seals, maybe. The rain has soaked down my hair, and I feel it seep through the shoulders

7

of my jacket. Duke, as big as he is, must be getting even wetter because he's only wearing that plaid shirt.

A gust of wind whips down the runway and nearly stops my forward progress for a moment.

"Sure you can fly in this weather?" I ask nervously.

"This is nothing," Duke replies. "Believe me."

I want to believe him. I'd also like to believe that he'll live to be eighty-six like C. D. Betts.

We pass about seventy-five planes before Duke stops next to a boxy blue one covered with dents, scrapes, and patches. It has big, fat oversize tires and looks as if it were built in someone's basement from spare parts.

"She's already loaded with Jake's supplies," Duke says, pulling a green tarp off the windshield. "I only get up there once every two or three weeks, so when I go I fly pretty heavy."

None of this makes me feel very good. "You sure we can't take a boat?"

"I told you not to worry," he says. "This here's an Air Force surplus Cessna with a Gopher 235 engine. She pulls her weight and more."

I just nod. I'm still not feeling reassured. I promised my mother I'd get to Uncle Jake's in one piece. *I'd hate to disappoint her.*

Duke unties the wings from the hooks in the runway that keep planes from being blown away in storms. We climb in and he starts pulling levers and twisting knobs. The plane's engine coughs and sputters, then stalls.

This does not make me feel really confident.

He tries again and finally gets the engine going.

Next to me Duke fills every inch on his side of the cockpit. He's busy flicking switches and adjusting handles and pull-cords. The inside of the Cessna looks even worse than the outside. The seats have been patched with so much silver duct tape that I can hardly find a trace of the original tan Naugahyde.

The throttle levers are worn smooth and shiny, and some of the toggle switches have broken off, leaving little stubs.

We taxi out to the runway. Duke starts pulling and pushing more levers, and the engine begins to whine.

"Ever been in a bush plane before?" Duke yells over the engine noise.

"No," I answer.

"Takeoff's a lot different than a jet."

"How?"

"Just strap on your seat belt tight and hold on," he advises. "You'll see."

The Cessna starts down the runway. The plane rattles and shakes. The single windshield wiper swipes back and forth, but the rain blurs the glass so fast it's practically useless.

We're picking up speed, but we still haven't left the ground. Peering through the windshield I manage to catch a glimpse of the end of the runway ahead. I can tell it's the end because a big pile of brown logs is lying there.

With each swipe of the wiper, those logs are getting closer.

And we're still not off the ground.

The logs are getting closer. . . .

I press my hands against the dashboard. This is seriously *not* funny. . . .

Whoa! At the last possible moment the plane lifts off, then rises swiftly as if it's being yanked upward by a big cord from above.

In the passenger seat I let out a long sigh of relief. When I look over at Duke, he's got a big smile on his face.

3

The plane climbs through the rain. The roar of the engine is loud inside the cockpit. The single windshield wiper swipes back and forth, giving us brief glimpses of fog ahead and a solid ceiling of gray clouds above.

Next to me Duke is still flicking switches and adjusting handles and pull-cords. A dozen dials and gauges on the dashboard jiggle and spin as we climb up under the clouds and then level off. Duke eases up on the throttle a little, but in my bones I can still feel the vibration of the engine.

Below us through the gray mist I catch sight of green tree-covered hills. No roads, no houses, no sign of civilization.

"Too bad you can't see Denali today!" Duke shouts over the roar of the engine.

"Denali?" I shout back.

"Indian name for Mount McKinley. Means the 'Great One.' Biggest mountain in the world."

"What about Mount Everest?"

"Everest is twenty-nine thousand feet above sea level at its peak, but the base of the mountain starts around 20,000 feet. Denali starts around 400 feet above sea level and rises to over 20,000. Compared to Denali, Everest is a runt."

Duke tips the plane's wings to give me a brief view through the mist of a wide gray river snaking through the hills and green forest.

"Tanana River!" he yells. "Biggest glacially fed river in the world. Whole north face of the Alaska range drains into it."

Biggest mountain. Biggest glacially fed river . . . *Texans must really hate this state.*

Sitting in the Cessna is like using one of those vibrating beds old motels have. It's fun for about a minute and then you can't wait for the shaking to stop. I hope we don't have too far to go, or my insides are going to start to resemble a milk shake.

"How long have you known Uncle Jake?" I ask.

Duke thinks for a moment. "Must be more than thirty years."

"Where'd you meet him?"

"Nam."

"Sorry?"

Duke gives me a sideways look. "Vietnam."

"I didn't know he was there."

Duke frowns. "You don't know him very well, do you?"

I shake my head. "Never met him. He's my mom's brother."

Duke just nods.

Outside, the clouds suddenly start to thin. Rays of sunlight break through, brightening little patches of brown and green on the rounded hills we're flying over. The plane begins to jolt a little.

"Wind currents around these domes get a little screwy," Duke says.

"Did you fly in Vietnam?" I ask. Duke said before he'd been flying for thirty-five years.

"Yeah, choppers."

"The kind that shoot rockets?"

Duke shakes his head. "The kind that carried boys a few years older than you into the jungle, and then came back later to pick up the pieces. Jake and I were what they called conscientious objectors."

"What's that?" I ask.

"Killing peasants halfway around the world from our country sort of went against our be-

13

liefs," Duke explains. "But we also felt strongly that we had to serve our country, so we trained as medics. I had some flying experience, so they made me a chopper pilot. . . .Hey, look at that!"

Duke banks the plane so sharply I have to grab the dashboard to keep from falling into him. The Cessna drops five hundred feet in about three seconds and starts to circle the top of one of the taller hills. Duke points at a large open field at the top of the hill. Near the center of it are three furry brown things—actually one large furry brown thing and two smaller ones.

"Grizzlies!" Duke yells.

I press my forehead against the plastic side window and feel it vibrate. At the sound of the airplane, the big grizzly stands up on its hind legs to get a better look at us.

"A sow and her cubs," Duke says.

"How do you know?"

"The males ain't much for baby-sitting."

We circle slowly. The mama grizzly is still standing on her hind legs, her big furry round head slowly turning, following us. Even though her fur is brown, when the sun hits it, it turns silverish.

"She can't see much," Duke says. "They get up on their hind legs and squint. Looks like they're mad as heck, but they're just trying to see."

"How do you know when they're really mad?" I ask.

"They get on all fours, with their ears cocked and their teeth grinding."

"Are there many of them where Uncle Jake lives?" I ask.

"Plenty," Duke answers.

4

"Couple of things you want to remember about grizzlies," Duke says. "First is they don't climb trees. Second, if you meet one and there are no trees around, don't run. Running suggests you're prey. And if a grizzly feels like it, he can run down a racehorse."

"So what do you do?"

"That's a good question. Some people say you should wave your arms and shout your lungs off at it. Sometimes the bear will stop and reconsider. Other people say you should throw your pack down and *then* run. If you're lucky, the bear'll find the pack more interesting than you. Especially if there's food in it. And another thing. I don't know if you'll ever catch anything with that rod of yours, but if you do, remember these animals have a fantastic sense of smell. They can smell sardines in an unopened can. Never wipe your hands on your clothes after handling fish. Burn your cans to kill the scent of food. And if you ever come across a fresh kill, get away fast because grizzlies don't like company when they eat."

Down on the ground it looks like Mama Grizzly doesn't like company, either. She's decided it's time to head for the trees. The cubs follow, looking like humpbacked dogs when they run.

"Darn shame," Duke mutters, more to himself than to me.

"What is?" I ask.

"We get a lot of tourists up this way," Duke answers. "They come to see Denali. Know what the number one attraction is?"

"No."

"Grizzlies. That's what they all want to see. Problem is, they've started to turn this place into a zoo. Lot of times they're careless, or just don't know any better. They'll leave food where the bears can get it. Even worse, they'll go ahead and feed 'em."

"What's wrong with that?" I ask.

"Ruins 'em. Turns 'em into rogues."

"The tourists?" I ask, puzzled.

Duke grins. "Naw, dummy, the bears. Once

17

they get a taste of human food, they tend to prefer it. All the sugars and junk. Anyway, it ain't long before they figure out that it's a lot easier to bust into a tent than it is to dig a ground squirrel out of its burrow."

"I'll remember that," I say with a nod.

"You better," Duke says. "Jake was just telling me they're having a problem with a rogue bear right now. Big fella, too."

We fly on for another fifteen minutes. The ride over the hills continues to be bumpy, and I'm glad I didn't have a big breakfast before we left. Finally Duke starts to descend. Below I can see a wide gray river. It must be the Kantishna. About a hundred yards inland from the river is a clearing with three cabins with sod roofs.

"That's Jake's place." Duke points down.

I look for some sign of human life, but don't see any. Duke turns the plane back toward the river.

"Wish he didn't live so darn close to the park," Duke mutters to himself.

I'm just about to ask him why when he dips the nose of the plane down sharply. It feels like he must be planning to land. Only I don't see anything that resembles a runway.

"Where do we land?" I ask.

"See that bar in the river?"

Down below I see a thin gravel sandbar in the

middle of the river. It can't be more than fifty yards long and no wider than a one-lane road. The plane continues to descend. We're twenty feet above the river now. Through the water I can see rocks on the river bottom as we race by above.

"You're gonna land on that bar?" I ask, just joking.

Duke nods. He's pretending to be serious.

"Oh, yeah, right." I smirk.

Duke glances at me out of the corner of his eye. "You want to see your uncle?"

I nod mutely.

"Then brace yourself."

5

Landing on the gravel bar is like snowboarding down an icy slope and then slamming into a patch of bare rock. The tires grab so suddenly that if it weren't for my seat belt I might go right through the windshield. Duke twists the steering wheel back and forth as the gravel bar disappears beneath us. Then the river races up. *Splash!* We jolt to a dead stop.

"Darn," Duke mutters.

I look out the window. The plane is sitting in about two feet of water. The gravel bar ended fifteen feet behind us. My heart feels like it's pounding a hundred miles an hour, and I take deep breaths to calm my nerves.

"You okay?" Duke asks.

"I guess."

Duke smiles and I look away, not wanting him to see that I'm shaken up. Out the window the river idles past. For the first time since I got to Alaska, the sun is starting to come out. Where the sunlight hits the water, it's hard to tell where the air ends and the liquid begins. I've never seen water so clear. The river looks pretty shallow and is about two hundred yards across. A thick, dark, green forest grows right down to its banks, and some huge spruces lean out at sharp angles over the water. It's total wilderness, not a sign of human life anywhere.

"Those boots better be back here," Duke grumbles as he reaches behind his seat.

I can't figure out why he didn't care about getting soaked by the rain back in Anchorage, but cares about getting his feet wet here.

"Maybe we should just roll our pants up," I suggest.

"Sorry, partner," Duke replies. "This river was froze up till a month ago. That's glacial runoff you're lookin' at. Otherwise known as ice water."

Duke finds a pair of dark green hip boots, then pushes open the door to give himself room to pull them on. He tells me to reach behind my seat where I'll find a hundred feet of braided red nylon climbing rope.

I reach back but don't feel anything like rope.

When I turn, I see the rope. I also see a big shotgun wedged into the back.

I grab the rope. With the boots on, Duke steps down into the water, then turns around and gestures to me with open arms.

"Come on."

"Come on what?" I ask.

"You don't think I'm pullin' this plane back on that bar by myself, do you?"

I climb out of the plane and Duke piggybacks me over to the gravel bar. Every time the sun comes out from behind a cloud, it's amazingly bright. I have to shade my eyes as I watch Duke wade back to the tail of the plane and tie the rope through an eyelet. Then he joins me on the bar, and together we pull on the rope with every ounce of strength we've got. The rope is stretched tight, our feet are sinking into the gravel, and the plane is slowly starting to inch backward. Now I understand the big tires. You couldn't land in places like this without them.

"Come on," Duke grunts as we pull and strain. "You're a big kid. Just a little farther."

It takes fifteen minutes to get the plane's tail halfway over the gravel bar, but that's good enough for Duke. He steps to the water's edge, slides open the cargo door, and throws my backpack in my direction.

"Set it down back there." He points at some light-colored dry gravel in the middle of the bar.

As I carry my pack up toward the dry spot, I take a closer look at the river. Except for the gurgle of the slowly moving water, it's very quiet. Suddenly out of the corner of my eye I see a fish leap and hit the surface with a splash. By the time I turn to look, all I can see are the widening ripples.

I turn back to Duke, who's lugging a large cardboard box toward the bar. "What kind of fish would break water in this river?"

Duke pauses to think. "Grayling, trout, salmon. You'll have plenty of time to admire the fish later. Right now we got work to do."

I take the box from him and set it down on the dry part of the bar. But I can't wait to go fishing.

As he continues to unload the plane, Duke hands me a couple of boxes of groceries, a twenty-five-pound jar of peanut butter, sacks of beans and rice, and a huge bag of cashew nuts. Then a large shiny frying pan, and a variety of machine parts a city boy like me wouldn't be familiar with. The last item is a heavy Army-green can with DANGER—FLAMMABLE/EXPLO-SIVE stenciled on the side.

"Explosives?" I ask. "The Fourth of July isn't for another month."

"It's just kerosene," Duke says. "Your uncle goes through a fair amount of this stuff."

"What for?"

"Ever seen an Alaskan mosquito?"

I figure he's pulling my leg. "Ha-ha."

Duke smiles back. "Wait till you see one. You won't think it's so funny."

6

We've just finished unloading the plane when the quiet is broken by the sound of an engine. Upstream a small skiff starts to make its way slowly toward us. The driver sits in the back, steering. Even from this distance I can see that he's clean shaven and has relatively short hair, brown in color. Like everyone else I've seen, he's dressed like a woodsman in jeans and a red plaid shirt.

The boat is fifty feet away now, and I can see the family resemblance. Like my mother, Uncle Jake's got a short forehead and a widow's peak and that famous Duvall jaw that makes people kid us about Dick Tracy. As the skiff comes closer he stares back at me. Where my mother

25

and I have blue eyes, his are light gray. Oddly, his skin looks pasty. I would have expected tan and rosy from all this sunlight and fresh air.

The nose of the skiff runs up onto the bar. Uncle Jake stands up slowly in the boat and puts his hands on his hips. He's lanky like my mother, but taller. I suddenly realize that what I thought was plaid is really a red shirt with dozens of patches. His jeans are also covered with patches.

"Tyler," he says with a smile.

"Uh, hi, Uncle Jake."

We shake hands. Meanwhile, the lines in Duke's forehead bunch up. "Jake, you feelin' okay?"

Uncle Jake turns to Duke. Spidery wrinkles at the corners of his eyes make him look like he's squinting. "Your landings are getting worse, Duke."

"Wasn't nothing wrong with that landing," Duke sputters.

"Your plane wound up in the river."

"Doesn't matter where my plane winds up," Duke replies. "If your stuff gets wet, *then* you've got something to complain about."

"As you say, Duke." Uncle Jake gazes at the supplies we've unloaded. "Better get this stuff over to the camp. You staying the night?"

Duke shakes his head. "Got to get back to Anchorage. Takin' some hunters up the Anaktuvuk Pass tomorrow."

Uncle Jake stares at Duke, and I can read the distaste in his face. "Trophy hunters." He spits the words out like bitter coffee.

"Don't start with me, Jake," Duke warns. "My job's to fly 'em in and out, not give 'em Sierra Club lectures."

"You could let some other pilot do it."

"I could starve, too," Duke says. "I don't see no one paying my gas up here today."

"I've got some money." I start to reach into my pocket.

"Put it away, Tyler," Uncle Jake says and turns back to Duke. "I thought you learned something outside Da Nang."

In disgust Duke throws his hands up in the air. "Darn it, Jake, I can't spend five minutes up here anymore without you gettin' on my case. Now I'm talkin' grizzlies, not human beings."

"They ain't that far apart," Uncle Jake says.

Duke just shakes his head. "Help me turn my plane around, Jake. So I can fly outta here before you lose the only friend you got."

Uncle Jake winks. "I love it when you talk pretty to me, Duke."

7

Well, I can't say I know what *that* was all about. But the next thing I do know, the three of us take the rope and start to pull the plane farther up on the bar. Uncle Jake's behind me, and when I glance at him, I notice that he's breathing hard and his face is quickly covered with sweat.

We turn the plane around. Then Duke climbs in and starts her up. The engine whines at full throttle and the plane begins to inch forward. The gravel bar is so narrow that Uncle Jake and I have to duck as the wings lumber past. Uncle Jake jogs up behind the plane and grabs the tail.

"Come on, Tyler," he grunts, digging his feet into the gravel as if he's trying to stop the plane from taking off.

He can't be serious, can he?

Looks like he is. I run up and join Uncle Jake holding the tail.

"What're we doing?" I yell.

"Giving him a little extra torque!" Uncle Jake yells back.

With our feet digging into the gravel, the plane moves sluggishly down the gravel bar. At this rate it looks certain that Duke is going to run out of gravel before he gets into the air.

"Let her go!" Uncle Jake suddenly grunts.

We let go and the plane lurches away, gradually picking up speed. Duke gets to the end of the bar and he's airborne, barely a foot or two above the river and slowly climbing.

Panting for breath, Uncle Jake and I stand on the bar and watch the plane climb into the sky and start to circle back toward us. Uncle Jake doubles over and rests his hands on his thighs like a tired basketball player. As Duke passes above us, he sticks his arm out the window and waves. Uncle Jake waves back. Despite the argument they just had, I get the feeling these guys mean a lot to each other.

"Duke's a good man," Uncle Jake says between gasps. "Just sometimes gets his priorities mixed up."

"Like how?" I ask.

"Flying sport-killers around."

"Hunters?"

Uncle Jake spits on the ground. "They're not hunters. They don't eat the meat or use the skins for clothing. They're just rich businessmen with fancy guns out on what they call an adventure. They kill a bear, take the hide, and leave the carcass to rot. They go home thinking they're heroes. When the day comes that all the grizzlies are gone, they'll be gone, too, so what do they care?" Uncle Jake shakes his head sadly. "Well, enough of that. Welcome to Alaska, Tyler. Let's get the skiff loaded."

We walk back toward the cargo Duke left on the bar. Together we start to load it into the skiff. Uncle Jake begins breathing hard. Soon he's wincing each time he tries to lift something heavy.

"Why don't you take a rest?" I tell him. "I can do it."

"All right." He sits down hard on the can of kerosene and grimaces.

"You okay?" I ask.

"Just been a little under the weather," he answers. "So how was your trip?"

"Piece of cake," I answer. "It's a direct flight from San Francisco to Anchorage."

"Sorry I wasn't at the airport to meet you," Uncle Jake says. "My kidney stones have flared up."

"What's that?" I ask.

"Nothing serious," he says. "Just something I get once in a while. Give it a couple of days and it'll go away."

I get the skiff loaded. Uncle Jake gets in, and together we head upriver. It's slow going. The skiff's only got a small five-horsepower motor, and it's weighed down pretty heavily with supplies. Heading up against the current I swear there are moments when we're not even moving. Believe it or not, you could probably walk faster.

Finally we make it to a sandy beach inside a small cove.

"Camp's about a hundred yards in along this trail." Uncle Jake points at a well-worn path into the forest. "You start off-loading and I'll go get the wagon."

He disappears down the trail, leaving me with the skiff. It takes me a while to unload all the cargo. This is the third time today I've handled most of these boxes, and I'm starting to feel a little bushed. By the time I finish, Uncle Jake still hasn't come back, so I sit on the kerosene can and wait.

Wilderness. When you sit still and listen, it's amazing how quiet it is. The river hardly makes a sound. The thick forest that grows right to the edge of the shore looks dark and foreboding. Maybe it's my imagination, but I get the feeling there are places very close to here where no human being has ever set foot. *Ever.* It's a spooky feeling, but peaceful, too. In most places quiet means no noise. Here, quiet seems to have a sound of its own. Suddenly I feel a million miles away from everything. It's a very lonely feeling. I'm awful far away from home.

Is this really what I wanted?

A tight ball of gnats hovers above my head and makes me wonder about those Alaskan mosquitoes Duke joked about. The sand on the shore around me is covered with animal tracks of all shapes and sizes. The animals must come to the river to drink. One set of tracks looks really big. When I get up and walk over to look at it, a fearful tingle runs up my spine. Each paw print is larger than both of my hands placed side by side. The sharp indentations in the sand above the toes mean long claws. I think back to that stuffed grizzly in the Anchorage Airport. I'm not even sure his claws were as big as the ones that made these tracks in the sand.

I raise my head and slowly look around. With the thick trees surrounding me, a bear could be ten feet away and I wouldn't even know it. I draw a deep breath and feel my heart beat nervously in my chest—a sensation not unlike the way you feel walking down a dark street in a bad neighborhood late at night.

8

So where's Uncle Jake?

A squeaking sound breaks the silence. It's coming from up the trail. A few seconds later someone comes around the bend pulling a gray wooden wagon, sort of like the wagons we played with as kids, only bigger and with taller sides. The wheels are making that squeaking sound. But Uncle Jake isn't pulling the cart. It's a kid dressed in patched clothes like Uncle Jake, but he's smaller, with dark skin and reddish brown curly hair.

He stops and stares at me. His skin is a brownish red, but his eyes are lidded like an Asian's. I would guess he's around my age. Could he possibly be Uncle Jake's kid?

Finally I step closer and offer my hand. "Hi, I'm Tyler."

He stares at my hand and then back at me. It takes a while, but he reaches out to shake.

"I am Richard," he says.

My dad taught me to shake hands firmly. Richard's handshake would've driven him crazy. It's like shaking hands with a warm dead fish. He won't look me in the eye, either.

Without a word he starts to search among the boxes and cans I brought ashore. The lines in his forehead are bunched up as if he's really bothered by something. Whatever he's looking for, it's not in the boxes. Next, he goes over to the skiff and looks through it.

Finally he looks at me. "You bring the mail?"

I shake my head.

"Duke did not give you the mailbag?" he asks.

Again I shake my head.

Richard purses his lips unhappily and starts to put the boxes into the wagon. I help him. It seems as if being in Alaska is a nonstop cycle of loading and unloading. Onto and off planes, boats, wagons, whatever. When the loading is finished, Richard goes around the front of the wagon to pull while I push from behind.

The forest is filled with unusual smells, but one stands out. It's some kind of animal smell, and it's strongest when we pass trees where silverish-brown balls of fur lay around the base. Some of the tree trunks have been stripped bare of bark. One trunk has deep, parallel grooves in it, as if someone cut into it with a power tool.

I stop pushing the wagon to take a closer look.

"Bear," Richard says.

"You've seen them around here?" I ask.

Richard nods.

"Up close?"

Richard nods more slowly and deeply. I feel a shiver.

Maybe I should have gone to Hawaii.

We work our way down the trail until we come to a clearing. Richard steers the wagon toward a square, boxy cabin with a sod roof. Steps lead up to a small front porch. It's made of old bleached gray logs with whitish stuff that looks like plaster in between the logs. The roof has grass growing on it and the windows on either side of the door are covered with filmy plastic. A rusty, blackened stovepipe juts out of the roof, and from it whitish smoke rises lazily into the sky.

The two other buildings in the clearing are more like huts, also built of logs.

A girl is sitting on the steps of the big cabin, playing with a doll. I'd guess she's six or seven years old. Her hair is straight and black, and her skin is darker than Richard's, but her eyes are like his. She stares mutely at me.

Uncle Jake comes to the door of the cabin. He still looks pale and unwell. "I see you two have met."

I give him a halfhearted shrug. Richard says nothing. He just stands there impassively.

"Richard and his sister Doris are from Unalakeet, about four hundred miles west of here on Norton Sound," Uncle Jake says. "On the Bering Sea."

Richard must not be into small talk because he says, "No mail."

Uncle Jake makes a face. "Aw, darn, that's my fault. I got so busy razzing Duke, I forgot to remind him. I'm sorry, Richard, guess we'll have to wait till next time."

Almost in slow motion Richard raises his hand to his mouth and starts to gnaw on his thumbnail. His eyes get narrow and dart back and forth like a squirrel feeding on a nut. I get the feeling he's really ticked about the mail not coming.

"Tyler," Uncle Jake says. "You and Richard better start unloading. Richard will show you where things go."

Off the airplane and onto the gravel bar. Off the bar and into the skiff. Out of the skiff and onto the shore. Off the shore and into the wagon. Out of the wagon and into the cabin. After this I hope I'll never have to touch any of these boxes again.

I expect to start taking the supplies into the house, but instead Richard pulls the wagon across the clearing to the base of a big tree. Bolted to the trunk is a crank with a metal cable—like the kind of thing that holds up the net on a tennis court. Richard starts to turn the crank and I look up. Coming down toward us is a wooden platform about six feet square.

The platform reaches the ground, and Richard pulls off the tarp. Under it are cans and cases of food.

"Uh, just out of curiosity," I say, "how come you keep this stuff up in a tree?"

"Bears," Richard grunts.

Richard and I start hauling the boxes off the wagon and onto the platform. Just when I'm starting to think that having a conversation with Richard is going to be totally impossible, he suddenly looks up at me and says, "You are from San Francisco?"

"Yeah."

"Someday I will go there," he says. "To the dog museum."

"Pardon?"

"The dog museum in San Francisco."

I don't know what to say. I've never heard of

a dog museum in San Francisco. Richard gives me that narrow-eyed suspicious look.

"You have heard of the dog museum?"

"Sorry, Richard, but I haven't."

"On Ashbury Street. You know that place?"

"Sure, I know Ashbury," I tell him.

Richard nods. "Then you know the dog museum."

Hello? Didn't I just say that I've never heard of it? What is with this guy?

Richard gives me a quizzical look, then looks away.

The conversation is over.

9

We finish loading the food supplies onto the platform. Richard reties the tarp and slowly cranks the platform back into the air. Just as he's finished, Uncle Jake comes out of the cabin again.

"You must be hungry after your trip, Tyler," he says.

I nod.

"Why don't you and Richard fix some dinner?" Jake says as we start toward the cabin. "I don't mean to sound inhospitable, but around here we all pitch in."

Sounds fair enough.

The door of the cabin is made of rough-hewn wood and must be three inches thick. The first thing I notice is that it's covered with long, deep parallel grooves. The same kind of grooves I saw on the tree in the woods. As I pass beneath a set of antlers that guards the entrance, and step inside, it occurs to me that there's no lock on the door, just a wooden handle. I guess that makes sense. They probably don't get many visitors up here.

Then again, maybe I'm wrong. Because as soon as we get inside, Richard picks up a thick wooden beam and lays it in two slots on the inside of the door. It reminds me of the way they reinforced castle doors in medieval times. With that beam across the door you'd need a battering ram to get in.

Inside, the cabin smells of propane gas. The logs in the walls are polished to a warm yellow color. The cabin actually looks larger inside than it did from outside. Just inside the door and to the right is a small kitchen area with a white porcelain sink. Above the sink are some rough wooden shelves stocked with jars, cooking utensils, plates, and spices. A rusty iron pot-bellied stove sits near the center of the front room. More shelves on the far wall are lined with hundreds of well-worn paperback books. On the floor in front of the shelves are piles of magazines. Some have been read so often that the pages are falling out.

I notice right away that there's no TV. Come to think of it, I didn't see a TV antenna or dish on the outside of the cabin.

And it's kind of doubtful they get cable way out here.

The kitchen table is made of mismatched planks of wood. The chairs are plastic milk crates. A cot is pushed up against the bare wall in the far right corner. Across the room are two other cots with several pairs of boots lined up under them. A couple of photos of racing cars are tacked on the wall above one of the cots. Above the other one is a poster of five cute little kittens all in a row.

Next to each cot is an old-fashioned wooden school desk and chair. A chessboard is set up on one of the desks, the pieces in neat rows, waiting to be moved.

"I'm just going to lie down for a moment," Uncle Jake says and goes through a door at the back of the cabin. I gather there's a bedroom back there.

Dinner consists of boiled hot dogs, string beans from a can, and instant mashed potatoes made with powdered milk. While I prepare the mashed-potato mix, Richard opens the can of string beans and Doris sets the table. Richard hasn't said a word since I said I'd never heard of the world-famous dog museum. Now I feel bad. I haven't been here an hour and already things are awkward. Maybe I can fix it up.

"Hey, listen," I tell him. "I really didn't mean to burst your bubble before. It's just that I've spent my whole life in San Francisco. When you're a little kid growing up in San Francisco, know what you do?"

Richard shakes his head.

"You go to museums. On every cold or rainy day you get dragged to some museum. First your school takes you. Then after school your baby-sitter takes you. Then on the weekends your parents take you because they're worried that if you stay at home, you're going to fry your brains on TV and video games. So I've probably been to every museum in San Francisco at least five times. Some of them I've been to dozens of times."

Richard gives me that serious look. "You never went to the dog museum?"

"Never."

"So you don't like dogs." Richard shrugs.

"It doesn't matter whether I like dogs or not," I tell him. "I never liked half the stuff they took me to see. You think I wanted to go to the folk art museum? The Museum of Colored Glass and Light? How about the piano museum? Boy, that was really interesting."

"The dog museum is there," Richard says

firmly. Then he turns away and pries the lid off the can of green beans.

Is it my imagination, or are things a little bit Loony Tunes up here in the wilderness?

When dinner's ready, we eat off dented metal plates and wash it down with Tang in dented metal cups. I must be pretty hungry because everything, even the string beans from the can, tastes good.

No one talks while we eat.

"Shouldn't we tell Uncle Jake that dinner's ready?" I finally ask.

Richard shakes his head.

"Should we bring him something?" I ask.

Again, Richard responds with a mute shake of his head.

Dinner's over. To my surprise, Richard tells Doris to do the dishes. I realize up here everyone has to pitch in, but little Doris looks as if she's pretty young.

"I'll help," I volunteer.

Richard shrugs as if he doesn't care.

So Doris and I do the dishes. Only there's no hot water in the cabin. In fact, there are no faucets. Next to the sink is a miniature hand pump, and when you pump it, icy cold water comes out. It must come straight from some underground spring.

Meanwhile, there's a big old black kettle always heating water on the wood-burning stove, and that's what we use for hot water to wash the dishes. Little Doris doesn't say a word the whole time. She just glances at me out of the corner of her eye now and then.

Why do I get the feeling this is going to be an interesting month? Filled with lively conversation with new friends? Yeah, right!

The dishes done, I suddenly realize how tired I am. It catches me by surprise, and for a moment I resist it because it's still light outside. Normally I don't go to sleep until it gets dark. Then I remember where I am, and check my watch. It's 11:30 P.M. I guess that's the thing about Alaska in the summer. With that sun out almost all of the time, you lost track.

I figure I'll lie down on the bare cot. It would be nice to have a sheet and blanket, but I'm so tired I don't even have the energy to go looking. I just lie down in my clothes and roll up my jacket for a pillow. Even though sunlight is still peeking in through the windows, I know I won't have any trouble falling asleep.

10

We're being attacked. Watch the flank!"

Someone's screaming. But it's not a dream. I sit up on the cot. It's still light out, and for a moment I'm totally disoriented. Is it day? Night? Where am I?

"He's shot! Get down! Down! I'm a medic! Darn it, Duke, where's the support?"

It's Uncle Jake. His screams are filled with so much terror they make the hair rise on the back of my neck. Across the room Richard's sitting up in his cot, too. In the cot next to him little Doris has pulled a pillow tightly over her head as if to block out the screams.

Richard's eyes meet mine for a second, then he looks away. I get the feeling he's heard this before.

"Duke? Duke! Where are you?" Uncle Jake cries.

After that it gets quiet again. Richard turns away and pulls his blanket over his shoulder. My heart's pounding and my mouth is dry. The clock next to Richard's cot says 3:08. I assume that's A.M. Outside it's sort of twilight. I slide back down on the cot and stare up at the log rafters that hold up the roof. I can't be sure, but it sounded like Uncle Jake's nightmare was about Vietnam . . . about being attacked. I remember what Duke said about flying in and picking up the remains. Only in Uncle Jake's dream, it sounds like Duke got there a little too late.

11

When I wake up the next morning, Richard and Doris are gone. Not only that, but their cots are neatly made. It seems strange that I not only slept through them getting up, but through them making their beds, too. Guess I must've been pretty tired. I sit up on my cot and stretch. Sunlight streams through the window, and the cabin feels quiet and empty. The door to Uncle Jake's room is closed. I wonder if he's gone, too. Maybe he's feeling better.

My stomach's grumbling. I feel hungry. Time to check out the refrigerator. Wait a minute, I just remembered there is no refrigerator. And no electricity, either. With the sun out nearly twenty hours a day I guess Uncle Jake doesn't need it. And what about in the winter when it's dark nearly all the time? That can of kerosene we brought on the airplane, plus a row of kerosene lanterns neatly lined up on a shelf against the wall answers that question.

In a cupboard by the sink I find some homemade bread and a jar of strawberry jam. No cereal, no eggs, no butter. The only milk is the powdered kind. A large jar of Tang provides 100 percent of my daily vitamin C requirements. You get the feeling that life up here is pretty lean.

I eat about five slices of bread and jam, and two glasses of cool refreshing Tang. Now a new sensation takes over. It's called find a bathroom.

I haven't seen anything that resembles a bathroom in the cabin. Of course, in the back is the door to Uncle Jake's room. There may be a bathroom in there, but I'm a little nervous about going in. Maybe it's private. Maybe Uncle Jake's still in there. On the other hand, if I don't find a bathroom soon, I'm going to have a big problem, so I knock really lightly.

When no one answers, I knock a little harder. Still no answer. I open the door and peek in.

Uncle Jake isn't there. I hope that means he's feeling better this morning. His room is kind of strange. He's lived here for twenty years, but it looks as if he just moved in. Except for one small bookshelf, the walls are bare. Nothing is out of place. The bed is made with military corners. A couple of pairs of boots are lined up beneath it. On top of the dresser are two small framed photographs. One is of two men with crewcuts in military uniforms. One man is tall and lanky, the other even taller, and husky. I give it a closer look. Yup, it's Uncle Jake and Duke, except they look a lot younger. The other picture I recognize right away. It's a photo of my grandparents. My mom has the same photo in her bedroom.

I'd like to stay and look around longer, but nature is calling and it's obvious there's no bathroom in Uncle Jake's room. Looks as if I'm headed for the great out-of-doors. I go out the front door of the cabin and down the steps and stop. The sun's so bright I have to shade my eyes with my hand. It feels pretty warm too, but right now I'm too busy thinking about other things to dwell on that. If there's no bathroom inside, there's probably one outside.

If I were an outhouse, where would I be?

If not in front of the main cabin, then around the side or in the back. I head around the side and *Violà!* there it is—a little wooden shack about the size of a closet. I lunge for it.

I'll spare you the gory details. Let's just say

this place gives new meaning to the phrase "roughing it."

I'm out of that outhouse as fast as possible. Once again I have to shade my eyes from the sun. It's very bright up here, and it's getting hot, too. Boy, that sun really makes a difference. When it's cloudy out, it's cool and chilly. With the sun out, you feel as if you're at the beach in Hawaii. Except for the slight rustling of leaves at the tops of some of the trees, there's no breeze. I have no idea where my uncle and the others are.

Remembering Uncle Jake's advice the night before, I go back into the cabin and straighten up my cot. I look around to see if there are any jobs that need doing, but I don't see any. I guess that means I can head for the river, where I hope it will be cooler and I can do some fishing.

I get out my sunglasses and fishing hat, my fly rod, reel, and flies. I'm in the process of packing up a bunch of bread and jam sandwiches and a big jar of Tang when the door opens and Uncle Jake comes in. He looks pale and gaunt, but maybe that's normal for around here. He stops and gives the fly rod a look, then goes over to the kitchen sink. "Sleep okay?"

"Yeah."

"I've been here twenty-seven years and I'm still not used to it," he says as he pumps some water into a big plastic glass and mixes himself some Tang. "You get used to the twenty-four hours of light in the summer. It's the winters that're hard to take."

"Because it's so cold?"

"Not just the cold, the dark."

"How come you came here?"

"Well, I got back from the war, and I guess I was pretty fed up with the human race." Uncle Jake carries the glass over and winces as he sits down slowly on one of the milk crates. "I just didn't want to have anything to do with them anymore."

Interesting. "How're you feeling?" I ask.

"A little better," he grunts.

"You sure?"

Uncle Jake blinks as if he's surprised I doubted him. Then he nods. "Yeah, I'll be fine." He rests the glass of Tang on his knee. There's a weary air about him.

"Hey, I almost forgot. I brought you some presents from Mom." I go over to my backpack and take out half a dozen oranges, a box of dried fruit, and a canned ham.

"That's nice of her," Uncle Jake says as I put the stuff in the kitchen.

"She would've sent more, but with all the rest of my junk, that was all I could manage," I explain.

51

Todd Strasser

"It's fine, Tyler," Uncle Jake says. "You okay with Richard and Doris?"

"What do you mean?" I ask.

"Richard asked you about the dog museum?"

"Yeah. What's that all about?"

"I'm not sure," Uncle Jake says. "It's something he picked up somewhere. He's pretty stuck on the idea."

"I get the feeling I shouldn't try to talk him out of it?" I ask.

Uncle Jake shakes his head. "Just let it be."

"I was wondering what the story is," I tell him. "I mean, Richard and Doris living with you. But if it's none of my business, you can just tell me to bug off."

"No, it's all right," Uncle Jake says. "There's not much to explain. They're just a couple of kids no one else wants. Until they got here, those two bounced around a lot."

"Why?"

Uncle Jake shrugs. "It's just the way it is for some kids. No one wants them, no one knows what to do with them."

"Don't they have parents?" I ask.

"Somewhere, I suppose."

"What happened to them?" I ask.

"What happened?" Uncle Jake repeats. "You and I came along, Tyler, that's what happened."

52

12

"What do you mean?" I ask.

"I mean, the white man came up here," he replies. "We took away their culture. We told them that they couldn't hunt whales and bears. We told them they had to go to school and learn algebra and English. These are people who've spent ten thousand years hunting and gathering and surviving without us to tell them what to do. And then we came along, and in the short span of a few dozen years we took away everything they had."

"Are they Eskimos?"

"Doris is. Richard's part Eskimo. His father was probably an American serviceman stationed up here. And they've never seen the inside of an igloo. Their people live in wood-and-sod houses. They're what you call a forest Eskimo."

That explains the totem pole I saw at the airport.

"What's with these desks?" I ask, gesturing at the school desks.

"Home schooling," Uncle Jake replies.

"No kidding?" I ask, interested. "You teach them?"

Uncle Jake nods. "What grade level do you think Doris is?"

"First, second? I don't know."

"Fifth," Uncle Jake says with pride. "How about Richard?"

"He looks about my age," I answer. "Sixth?"

"Tenth," Uncle Jake says with a smile. "You play chess?"

"Matter of fact, yes," I answer, not bothering to add that I'm on my school's chess team.

"You might want to ask Richard to play," Uncle Jake says.

"Sure."

My uncle takes another gulp of Tang and licks his lips. "Good day to do some fishing."

"Yeah."

"Probably a lot cooler by the river."

"That's what I'm thinking."

"Know how to handle an outboard?" he asks.

That catches me by surprise. "Well, sure, but

I can fish from the shore. I mean, that boat's your only form of transportation."

"I hear the fishing's best out in the middle," he says.

"You've had some luck there?" I ask.

"No." He shakes his head. "It's just what I've heard."

"You don't like fish?" I guess.

"Love it," he answers. Then off my scowl he adds, "But so do the bears."

I nod. "Gotcha."

"Weren't planning on bringing any trophies back here, I hope," he says.

"No problem," I answer. "I'm strictly catch and release anyway. Most of the time I can get the hook out without even taking 'em out of the water."

"Good." Uncle Jake nods. "If you do wind up handling any fish, make sure you don't wipe your hands on your clothes. Take some soap and wash your hands in the river."

"Will do."

Uncle Jake grins. "The other thing to remember is this side of the river's open to anyone, but officially, the other side is part of Denali National Park."

"And there's no fishing allowed in national parks?" I guess.

"Smart boy. Have fun."

"Thanks." Loaded with my gear, sandwiches, and jar of Tang, I head out.

"Tyler?" Uncle Jake calls behind me.

"Yeah?" I stop and turn.

"Just one other thing. The river gets pretty shallow in spots. You have to watch for the rocks or you'll bust the prop."

"I'll keep it in mind." I wave and head down the trail to the river.

The sun in the clearing feels like a sauna, so I don't mind being in the shade of the woods. I've never been a real observer of nature. But out here you can't help noticing how untouched and fresh everything feels. A canopy of trees covers the trail like brown and green arches of a Gothic cathedral. The trees are mostly tall pine needle spruces, but here and there is an occasional stand of paper birches with peeling white bark.

It's a shame to think that given enough time, we'll probably destroy all this, too.

Soon I see the Kantishna through the trees, and moments later I break through to the riverbank. The Kantishna moves wide and lazy, its rocky bottom as clearly visible as the nose on my face. The *rat-a-tat-tat* of a nearby woodpecker gives rhythm to the day, and with the sun on the water the river turns a shade of hazy apple green. Above me is a broad expanse of blue sky with small white cumulus clouds evenly spaced, sort of like a blue-and-white checked tablecloth.

I stow everything in the skiff and pull on the engine cord. The little outboard starts right up. I steer from the back, twisting the grip on the outboard's metal arm to give it more gas as the skiff glides into the river. With just me in it, the skiff floats higher in the water and moves faster, though not very fast at all compared to other boats I've been in. Here and there a small boulder sticks out of the water, but I'm careful to give them wide berth.

Out in the middle of the river are the deep spots where the fish are more likely to rest. I find one particularly tempting spot and anchor the skiff upstream from it. Since I'm not sure what kind of fish I'm going to encounter, I start by tying a streamer called a Gray Ghost on my line. It's a large fly that looks like a big fat water nymph and should be tempting to any hungry fish that comes across it. I stand up in the skiff, make about a dozen casts, and come up empty. It's time to try a different place.

Along the opposite shore and another twenty-five yards downstream a big spruce log lies sideways in the river, wedged there by rocks. The water on the other side of the log looks pretty calm and would be the perfect place for a fish to lie in wait for food. I know that's the park side of the river, but as long as I'm not on the shore I figure no one will mind.

Actually, what I really figure is that no one will know.

I start the outboard, pull the anchor, and head for the log. I anchor about ten yards from the shore. The water here looks only a few feet deep.

I cast the streamer. It hits the flat surface of the water with a light *plop!* and I let it sink a bit and then begin to tug it slowly back upstream, hoping to make it resemble a newly hatched nymph swimming along the bottom.

Suddenly the line goes tight. For a second I think I've snagged a tree branch, but then the fish starts to run. The next thing I know, line is streaming off my reel. I don't know what I've got, but from the way my rod is bending and the sound of the line screaming off the reel, this has to be the biggest fish I've ever hooked.

The fish heads downstream like an express train. There's no way I can stop it or turn it around without snapping the line, so the only chance I have is to follow it. But I can't do that and steer the boat at the same time.

Meanwhile, line continues to stream off the reel. I'm almost down to the backing.

If I don't do something fast, I'm going to lose the biggest fish I've ever hooked.

I look down into the clear water beside the boat. You can see the smooth, round rocks on the bottom. It can't be more than two feet deep.

The reel is down to the backing, but this fish has shown no signs of stopping. If I don't do something fast it's going to break the line. I'll never even get to see what it is.

Or how big it is.

Unless . . .

Holding my bent rod in one hand and grabbing my day pack with the other, I jump.

Splash!

Yeow! Duke was right. I've never been in water so cold. My feet go numb almost immediately. Fish or no fish I can't stay in this ice water for long. I start downriver, angling toward the gravel shore. Just ahead of me, leaning over the river, is a white birch. I grab it and pull myself up on the bank with one hand while holding the rod with the other. As I climb back onto dry land again, the fish reaches the end of the backing on my reel.

The rod curls like a big letter C and then . . . *Pop!*

Everything goes slack.

After all that, my line snapped.

I stand on the riverbank shaking the water out of my pants and shoes.

Believe it or not, I'm not that disappointed.

Totally psyched is more like it. I just hooked the biggest fish of my life. Sure I would've liked catching it, but that's not the point. The point is, for a little while that fish and I were connected, we were in a battle. The fish won and I respect that. Fly-fishing isn't about putting meat on the table. It's not about killing some beautiful living creature. It's about battle, and may the best man or fish win. I would have let that fish go anyway.

And now I know why Duke seemed so amused by my fly rod. That fish was way too big and strong. If they're all like that, I may never get to land one. But I'll have a great time trying.

I walk back up the shore until I'm parallel with the skiff, which is still anchored in the river. About twenty-five feet of frigid water separates us. But I'll have to wade through it to get back to the skiff. Can't say I'm looking forward to it. I'm only now getting the feeling back in my feet. Well, there's no rush. In fact, all the excitement has given me an appetite. So why not sit down on the shore and have a snack? Sure, I'm on park property now, but am I fishing?

Nope.

Once again, the sun is amazingly bright and hot. I find a spot on the shore under a spruce where I can sit with my wet legs in the sun and the rest of my body in the shade. I open my pack and pull out a bread-and-jam sandwich.

I eat the sandwich and drink some of the Tang. On the ground around me is a heavy blanket of dried brown pine needles. I pick one up and start to twist it between my fingers. It's longer than any pine needle I've ever seen around San Francisco, but that fits Duke's description of Alaska. Biggest mountain, biggest glacier-fed river, biggest pine needles. Looking out across the river, I can see the other shore, and the forest beyond it, and huge snowcapped mountains beyond that. It's an amazing sight. I still can't believe I'm really in Alaska.

Then I hear something in the woods behind me that makes me think maybe I can believe it after all.

Crunch!

13

I twist around.

Standing in the woods no more than forty feet away is the biggest bear I have ever seen, in or out of a glass display. On its hind legs it must be twelve feet at least.

A shiver of ice-cold fear grips me from head to foot.

Don't move! Wasn't that what Duke said? Well, it's not hard. Right now I'm so darn scared I *can't* move!

The bear is up on its hind legs. Turning its head, squinting and sniffing as if it smells something but can't see exactly what.

"Some people say you should wave your arms and shout your lungs off at it."

Oh, sure. Piece of cake. Right now my throat is so frozen with fear I can hardly breathe, much less shout.

Thump! I actually feel the ground shake as the bear drops back down to all fours. It starts toward me!

"Other people say you should throw your pack down and run. If you're lucky, the bear'll find the pack more interesting than you. Especially if there's food in it."

My pack has those bread-and-jam sandwiches in it. And a pack of peanut M&M's.

Here goes nothing!

I quickly stand up and dump out my pack.

The bear freezes. Its ears stand up, along with all the silvery-brown hair on its back. In a flash it snarls, revealing those teeth, then makes a weird growl.

And charges.

14

*S*tand still and yell at it?

You'd have to be out of your mind.

I turn and run into the water toward the skiff, splashing like mad and expecting at any second to feel this monster grab me from behind.

It's not until I've thrown myself into the skiff that I dare look back and see that the bear has indeed stopped at my pack and is scarfing down my sandwiches, plastic bags and all.

I clamber to the back of the skiff and give the cord a yank. The outboard coughs to life. On the shore the grizzly lifts its head and squints. Its ears go back up. There's still only about twenty-five feet of shallow water between us. I pull the anchor, twist the grip, and steer for the deeper water. Back on shore the bear hasn't budged. I catch a glimpse of something yellow in its paws. It must be the bag of peanut M&M's.

As much as I love those candies, I guess this is a good time to learn to share.

15

It isn't until I get back to Uncle Jake's side of
the river that I realize I not only left my pack,
but my fly rod, too. I feel like a jerk. I mean,
not that anyone actually *warned* me not to go
over to that side of the river. Uncle Jake only
said it was national park and therefore I
shouldn't fish.

As I tie up the boat and head up the trail
toward the cabin, the following questions float
into my head:

1) Do I tell Uncle Jake what happened?
*No, because if I do, he might not let me go
back across and get my fly rod.*

2) Do I really *want* to go back across and get my fly rod?
Well, not if the bear's going to be there. On the other hand, the bear has to move on, doesn't he? And I did come here to fish. Otherwise, it's going to be a pretty boring visit.

So I figure I won't say anything. Maybe they won't even notice that I don't have my rod or pack. Then tomorrow I'll take the skiff back across the river and grab my rod *very quickly*.

And that'll be the end of it.

I come to the cabin and cross the porch. Inside, Richard's standing at the kitchen sink and Doris is over by her cot playing with her doll. The cabin has a different scent. I can't say I've ever smelled it before, except that it's sort of herbal. Over at the sink Richard is pouring steaming water from the kettle into a teapot.

"Where's Uncle Jake?" I ask.

"In his room," Richard answers.

"Is everything okay?" I ask.

Richard shoots Doris a look, then turns to me and nods down at the teapot.

"Richard?" That's Uncle Jake's voice from his room. He sounds like he's in complete agony.

Richard picks up the teapot and crosses the cabin. He opens Uncle Jake's door, then quickly shuts it behind him as if he doesn't want me peeking in.

But I can still hear every agonized groan from my uncle's lips. *"Richard, in the top drawer of my dresser. A brown bottle of pills."*

Sheesh! He sounds as if he's in really bad shape!

A few moments later Richard comes out of the room, looking grim. If I can hear everything Uncle Jake says, it means he can probably hear everything I say, too.

"You *sure* he's okay?" I whisper.

Richard nods.

"He's been through this before, right?" I whisper hopefully.

Again, Richard shoots Doris a look. You can tell something's going on here. "Yes," Richard answers with a nod.

But just then we hear a rattling sound followed by a small crash, then another groan from Uncle Jake. It sounds as if the teapot fell to the floor. Richard hurries back into the room, once again closing the door behind him. Left alone in the main cabin with me, Doris hugs her doll fearfully.

More moans come from Uncle Jake's room, followed by Richard nervously trying to reassure him. "You will be okay. Drink this. You will get better."

Somehow I get the feeling that whatever's wrong with Uncle Jake, it's not only *not* getting better, it's worse than usual.

A little while later Richard comes out again. He's chewing the skin on the side of his thumb and looking every bit as worried as before. He goes over to the sink and soaks a small towel in cold water, then wrings it out and heads back to Uncle Jake's room.

"Can I see him?" I ask in a low voice.

Richard shakes his head. Like he's some kind of nurse. But I can't argue with him. He lives here. I'm just a guest.

Time passes. Doris sits on her cot, hugging her doll and saying nothing. Every once in a while I hear Uncle Jake moan. Every now and then Richard comes out, rewets the towel in the kitchen sink, then goes back into Uncle Jake's room.

It isn't long before I'm starting to feel hungry again. It must be the fresh Alaskan air and all the excitement. Since Richard's busy with Uncle Jake, I take it upon myself to cook dinner.

The choices aren't great. There's bread, instant mashed potatoes, powdered milk, and odd cans of vegetables, gravy, and soup. I get the feeling they keep most of their food supplies on that platform in the tree, but I don't want to

bother Richard about lowering it now. He's got
his hands full with my uncle.

Then I remember the ham Mom sent up, and
it gives me an idea. Suppose I heat up the ham
and serve it for dinner with mashed potatoes,
gravy, and peas? It sounds practically gourmet.

16

The next step is getting Doris into the act.

"Hey, you want to help me cook dinner?" I ask.

She just blinks at me.

"Come on." I wave her over. "I'm gonna give you something hard to do. Like add water to the mashed-potato mix."

It takes some coaxing, but I finally get Doris over to the sink. She even giggles when I give her an empty milk crate to stand on so that she can reach the water pump.

While Doris works on the mashed potatoes, I slice the ham and then start to heat it in a skillet on the woodstove.

Doris needs to measure out the right amount

of water for the potatoes, so I figure she'll need a little help with the measuring cup.

"Here's how it works," I start to explain. "There are two cups in a pint and two pints in a quart. So of course you'd figure there'd be two quarts in a gallon, right? Well, that would be too logical. So instead, there are—"

Doris just rolls her eyes at me like I'm a total dummy. Then she takes the cup and measures out exactly what's needed.

"Oh, right." I grin sheepishly. "Uncle Jake said you were on a sixth-grade level."

In the middle of all this blathering, something behind us has started to sizzle, but it doesn't dawn on me that it's the ham until I smell smoke.

Darn!

I grab the skillet from the stove. Smoke's billowing out of it, but I don't think the ham's too badly burned, and I don't want to dunk it in the sink and ruin the meat. Instead I find a big metal platter and smother it.

Of course by now the cabin's full of ham smoke, so I open the windows. Then I lift the wood beam and open the door to get some fresh air. I stand in the doorway waving a dish towel to push the smoke out.

"Come on, Doris! I need your help!"

Doris hurries over and we stand together in

the doorway waving. She actually smiles up at me. I have to admit that it makes me feel good.

We've just about gotten the smoke out of the cabin when Richard comes out of Uncle Jake's room. He stops short and sniffs the air. His eyebrows rise with alarm as he takes in the scene: the open windows and door, the skillet with the slightly burned ham.

The lines in his forehead bunch up as he races past Doris and me and goes outside.

What's this all about? I wonder, following him. Outside, Richard stops and stares upward. I stop beside him. It takes me a moment to figure out that he's looking at the smoke coming out the old stovepipe in the roof.

As the smoke rises up into the air, it begins to drift toward the river.

"It goes to the park," he mutters, and then turns to me. "Go inside, keep the door closed."

17

I don't see what Richard is so concerned about. If he's worried that a bear might smell the smoke, he seems to be forgetting that we're separated from the park by the river, which is wider than a soccer field. And even though it isn't the deepest river I've ever seen, there are spots where the bottom has to be at least twelve feet down.

Back inside the cabin Richard secures the front door and closes the windows. We eat my ham and mashed-potato dinner, which, by the way, is pretty good if I do say so myself.

Richard eats in silence. I wonder if there's a way to get him to open up. Then I remember the chessboard.

"Want to play chess?" I ask.

Richard straightens up and nods eagerly.

Next thing I know, we're sitting at the chessboard. Like I said, I'm on my school's chess team, so I figure I'll go easy on him.

Fifteen moves later I'm staring at the board in disbelief.

"Checkmate," Richard says with a smile.

No, it's not possible! I haven't been beaten that fast since I was eight!

"Play again?" Richard asks.

"Better believe it," I answer. This time I'm going to use an opening he's never seen before. The grand masters use it. One of my teachers taught it to me.

So this time it takes twenty-three moves for him to beat me.

"Checkmate!" Richard loves this. "Play again?"

I nod. This time I'm *really* going to concentrate.

He wins in twenty-one moves.

I just sit there staring at the board. *This kid is a genius!*

Meanwhile, Richard keeps stealing glances at me. You can almost see his mind working. I just keep smiling and nodding back, trying to give him a sign that whatever he's wondering about, it's okay to ask me.

"You have heard of Balto?" he finally asks.

"Balto?" I frown.

Richard looks disappointed. You get the feeling that now he's going to clam up.

"Tell me," I encourage him. "I want to know."

"Balto was the lead dog for the serum sled to Nome," Richard says, then pauses and studies me. "You have heard of this?"

"Can't say that I have, Richard."

Richard looks at me with a raised eyebrow. "Many years ago there was a smallpox epidemic in Nome. The serum was in Anchorage, a thousand miles away. It had to go by sled. Balto was the lead dog, all the way to Nome. He saved many lives."

Suddenly this actually rings a bell in my mind. "Wait a minute! Isn't there a sled race from Anchorage to Nome that has something to do with that?"

"Yes!" Richard nods eagerly. "The Iditarod. It is the same path Balto took. It is a race to honor Balto."

"So this dog Balto is famous?"

Richard keeps nodding, suddenly all excited and talkative. "Getting through the blizzard was a miracle."

"But there hasn't been any smallpox in years. Balto can't still be alive."

Richard shakes his head. "In the dog museum."

Oh, no, we're back to that. Balto, the stuffed pooch in the world-famous dog museum.

Once again I wonder if it's possible that I grew up in San Francisco and somehow missed this dog museum. That I got taken to every museum in San Francisco, *except* the dog museum.

No, I'm really sorry, but this is simply not possible.

"Let me ask you something, Richard," I say as gently as I can. "Who told you about this dog museum?"

Richard stops smiling. "A man."

"A man?" I repeat.

"He knew my grandfather."

"So?"

"They took Balto when my grandfather was a boy."

"And why's it so important for you to see Balto?" I ask.

Richard puffs out his chest proudly. "Balto was my great-grandfather's dog. I will go to the dog museum to see him."

Suddenly I get this sick feeling in my stomach. You think about the kind of upbringing Richard had. The kind of people he might have been around. Is it possible that someone was pulling Richard's leg? I'm 99.9 percent sure there's no dog museum in San Francisco. And if there was, why would they send Balto there? Wouldn't the Alaskans want to keep him in Alaska? I can just picture this kid going his whole life clinging to this idea that someday he'll go to San Francisco to see Balto in the dog museum.

And it's all someone's idea of a joke.

A very sick joke.

Richard may be a genius, but he doesn't know a lot about the real world.

We hear a groan from Uncle Jake's room. Richard goes to see how he's feeling while Doris and I do the dishes.

It isn't long before we're finished. Now what? Doris and I sit on our cots and do nothing. Every fifteen minutes, Richard comes out of Uncle Jake's room and rinses the hand towel. It's weird how he won't let Doris or me go back there and see my uncle. What does he think we'll do?

Doris and I wait. It's evening now, but you'd never know it. Outside it still looks like afternoon. I'm starting to feel cooped up inside. It is totally amazing to me that they live up here without a TV. What do they do at night or in the winter?

I guess that's why all the magazines and paperbacks look so worn out.

It would be nice to go for a walk. Even if Richard doesn't want to come, I could take Doris. We could go down to the river and skip stones or build a little raft out of sticks and watch it float away.

Thump! A sound comes from the porch.

What was that?

Thump! There it is again. It's like a heavy footstep on the front porch. It *felt* like it, too. The floor in the cabin actually shook.

Richard comes out of Uncle Jake's room. He stops in the middle of the cabin and stares at Doris and me, pressing his finger to his lips.

Be silent. Don't move.

We freeze. You can hear the faintest hiss as steam escapes from the kettle on the woodstove. And a tiny *splat* as a drop of water falls from the pump faucet into the sink.

Creak! On the front porch, wooden planks creak. Now we can hear loud sniffs outside.

I've heard that sound recently. Like just a few hours ago on the other side of the river. Sniffs from a nose attached to about six hundred pounds of hungry bear.

The door rattles and we hear a scrape as if a bear is scratching at the wood. I get the distinct idea that he's feeling his way around, looking for an opening.

Creak! Thump! Thump! These next sounds

surprise me. It sounds as if the bear has turned away from the door and gone back across the porch and down the steps.

The seconds pass. I can feel my heart pounding.

Still nothing from outside.

A sense of relief washes through me. "Is he gone?" I ask.

Richard turns quickly and shakes his head.

Crash! A huge, *wet,* furry bear arm smashes through a window, shattering the glass.

18

The bear is reaching into the cabin. At the end of its furry wet arm, the amazingly long claws swish back and forth through the air. It must be trying to grab anything it can. The wet fur throws off a spray.

Looks as if that bear decided to swim across the river after all.

Crash! With a swing of his arm, he rips a shelf of dishes and cups right off the wall.

Inside the cabin, Richard, Doris, and I watch in shocked silence. The bear swings his arm again but, feeling nothing else, soon pulls his arm back out.

The next thing I know, his huge head appears in the window. It's like that scene in *King Kong* when the big ape looks in through the window at that lady, except the bear's head isn't *that* big. Just about twice the size of a basketball.

Grrrrrr! The bear snarls and bares his huge white teeth.

Doris screams and grabs Richard around the waist.

Thunk! The bear tries to force his head into the window, but the frame is too small.

Thunk! He backs off and charges again, growling and snarling as he tries to shove his head in.

The logs around the window shift and shake. That white plaster-like material in the spaces between the logs begins to crack and fall away.

Thunk! The bear slams his head into the window frame again as if he's using it as a wedge or battering ram. The logs squeak and shake some more.

Is it possible that he could smash his way right through the wall?

Until this moment Richard, Doris, and I have watched, transfixed. As if none of us believes this is really happening. But when the logs around the window begin to creak and give, Richard swings his head around as if looking for something. He heads for the kitchen area and yanks open a drawer, pulling out a medium-sized knife.

He heads for the bear. On one hand, it's a

courageous act of bravery. On the other hand, in order to use the knife he's going to have to get awfully close to that monster.

"Wait!" I shout, grabbing the kettle of boiling water off the stove and flinging it into the bear's face.

With a screeching howl, the bear backs away from the window. Richard nods at me as if he's very glad I've spared him the task of attacking that bear with the knife. But now I've got another idea and grab the kitchen broom.

Richard gives me the funniest look, as if he thinks I mean to sweep up the broken glass from the window. "Tie the knife to the broom handle," I explain. "We can use it like a spear to keep him away."

"What the devil's going on?" It's Uncle Jake, propping himself up in the doorway to his room. His skin is beyond pale; it's gray. And his eyes have a sickly, sunken look.

"Bear!" Richard answers as he opens the kitchen drawer and pulls out a ball of twine.

Thunk! Grrrrrr! The bear slams into the window frame again. The logs around the frame shudder and creak, but Richard's only begun to lash the knife to the broom pole.

"Pepper, Tyler," Uncle Jake says in an amazingly calm voice.

Good idea. In a spice rack in the kitchen I find a tin of pepper and pour a heap into my hand.

Ha-choo! Almost instantly I sneeze and blow the pepper out of my hand.

Grrrrr! The bear growls and the logs around the window quake as he keeps trying to push his way in.

"Try again!" Uncle Jake urges me.

Wait a minute! I turn and stare at my uncle. "Don't you have a gun?"

"No," my uncle replies. "Now use the pepper!"

Holding my breath, I pour another heap into my hand, then step toward the bear and fling it.

The bear snorts and backs away from the window. Outside he sneezes and shakes his head repeatedly.

It might actually be funny if he wasn't intent on killing and eating us.

"Think that'll do it?" I ask hopefully inside the cabin.

"Not a prayer," Uncle Jake answers.

"You've been through this before?" I ask.

Uncle Jake shakes his head. "Nope."

"Then how do you know?" I ask.

"I know bears. I've watched them for twenty years," Uncle Jake replies grimly. "And what I haven't seen myself, I've heard stories about. They don't give up easy."

"Maybe this one will—"

Crunk! I don't have time to finish the sentence. The bear smashes into the window frame again, growling and snarling.

Richard quickly finishes the broom-handle spear and jumps up to charge.

"Not from the front!" Uncle Jake orders. "From the side!"

Richard changes course and heads for the wall.

"Jab him hard and then pull back fast!" Uncle Jake instructs in that calm steady voice. "Don't let him take the spear!"

Richard jabs the bear in the side of the head and then pulls back. The blade comes out smeared red. The bear lets out a doglike howl and then quickly retreats.

Except for our heavy breaths, the cabin slowly becomes quiet.

"That'll hold him for a bit," Uncle Jake slides down into a sitting position on the floor.

19

But for how long? How long until the bear comes back?

"It won't be long," Uncle Jake mutters. "Help me up, boys."

Richard and I hurry over to the doorway. We help him stagger over to Doris's cot, where he sits down hard, panting for breath. "Richard, get me four more of those pills and some water."

For some reason, Richard shakes his head.

"Do it!" Uncle Jake shouts with a burst of anger that catches us all off guard.

Richard dutifully gets the pills and the water.

"Feeling any better?" I ask.

Uncle Jake shakes his head and looks pale

and grim. "I don't mean to worry you, Tyler, but it's never been this bad."

"Well, I hate to say this, but I *am* worried," I answer. "I'm a million miles away from home. You're really sick, and there's a huge bear out there that wants to kill us. What's with that thing anyway?"

"It must be that rogue from the other side of the river," Uncle Jake says, shaking his head. "Can't imagine what would bring him all the way over here."

Richard and I share a look. Sounds as if the seared ham did it. Is Richard going to tell? He looks away.

"Can't we call for help?" I ask.

"Not yet," Uncle Jake answers.

"Excuse me for asking, but what are we waiting for?" I ask.

Uncle Jake shovels the pills into his mouth, takes a sip of water, and throws his head back to swallow. "It's Richard and Doris. They're not here legally, Tyler. They're here because . . . well . . . no one else wants them and they've got no place else to go. You bring a rescue situation in here, and someone's bound to ask what's going on."

"So why can't you just make it legal?" I ask.

"Because legally they're both supposed to be with some foster family that just wants 'em for the extra income," Uncle Jake explains. "Now, I'd love to engage in a philosophical conversation about the pros and cons of the foster care system in this country, but you boys have some work to do before that bear comes back. First thing you've got to do is shore up that window."

"How?" I ask.

Uncle Jake thinks for a moment and then says, "Richard, get out the hammer, saw, and pry bar. And all the nails you can find. Go into my room and bust the counter off my dresser. It'll be just about the right size to fit over the window."

Richard and I do as we're told. It isn't long before we come back with the counter from the dresser.

"Okay, good," Uncle Jake says. "Now hammer it up over the window."

I hold the countertop while Richard hammers it.

"Excuse me for saying this," I interrupt while we work, "but that bear seemed awful strong. What'll stop him from just pushing this piece of wood in?"

"Nothing," answers Uncle Jake. "And that's why you're going to go back into my room and pry up a couple of floorboards and use them for reinforcement. And that means covering up the other windows, too."

Richard and I do as we're told. Prying up and sawing the floorboards is hard work. I've lost track of time, but I know it must be late. Even though I'm running on pure adrenaline, I feel tired, too.

"Hurry, boys," Uncle Jake urges us as we work.

"You were really calm before," I mention to my uncle while I hold a board and Richard saws.

"Yeah, well, I'll admit that bear's pretty scary," Uncle Jake answers. "But I saw worse in Nam. And I learned there that panic is as bad an enemy as you can face."

"And you're sure he'll be back?" I ask. "I mean, the bear."

"I'm not sure of anything," my uncle answers. "You know what a rogue bear is, Tyler?"

I swallow and nod. "Yes."

"Well, a rogue bear in the early summer is about the worst combination there is," Uncle Jake explains. "That big fellow has just come out of hibernation, and he's mighty hungry. Trouble is, it's early summer here and there's not a lot of edible vegetation around yet. That's why the majority of grizzly attacks on large animals come in the late spring and early summer when they're desperate and looking for a big meal."

"And when you come right down to it," I reply,

"to a grizzly we're basically not much more than a big meal."

"That's right."

"I guess you know that's not very reassuring," I mope.

"Well, I think it's best if you understand what's driving this creature," Uncle Jake says. "It's not an enemy. It's just a hungry animal working it's way up the food chain."

I'll have to remember that the next time one tries to eat me.

"So, if he's hungry and desperate for food, why doesn't he attack again?" I ask.

"Because he's smarting," Uncle Jake answers. "We stung him good and he knows it."

"I'm just curious," I tell him. "But do you think this bear's smart enough to know humans did it? I mean, is he smart enough to get mad?"

"Oh, yeah." Uncle Jake nods solemnly. "You better believe it."

20

Two A.M. The sun's just below the horizon, so it's sort of dusk out. Doris has fallen asleep on Richard's cot. Richard has gone into Uncle Jake's room to lie down. I can't believe that he'll really be able to sleep. Meanwhile, Uncle Jake hasn't moved from Doris's cot. He sits there, looking pale gray, his forehead damp with sweat. Every now and then he winces.

"Jeez, I'm gettin' too old for this," he groans.

"Anything I can do?" I ask.

He shakes his head.

"Shouldn't we do something?" I ask.

"Not much we can do," he answers.

"But if the bear's gone . . ."

"It's too soon to know," he says, then grimaces.

"I just hate seeing you in such pain," I tell him.

He looks up at me and forces a smile on his face. "Tell me something, Tyler, because no one else around here will. Do I go on about that Vietnam stuff too much?"

"Not yet," I answer.

"Okay, then here's what I think about pain," he says. "My platoon got stuck on top of a hill. There wasn't a thing up there. The whole hill had been defoliated. It was just some broken tree trunks, sticks, dead grass, and mud. And there we were, surrounded by the North Vietnamese. And I had shrapnel in my leg, my butt, my back, and one nasty little piece behind my ear. We sat up there for fifty-three hours. Fifty-three hours bleeding, hungry, thirsty, and in a lot more pain than I am right now."

"And then what?" I ask.

"Air support came in and scattered the enemy," Uncle Jake says. "Then Duke evacuated us. I spent time in the hospital in Saigon, then collected my Purple Heart and came home."

I look at my watch. "Well, I figure that means we've got about forty-six hours to go."

"Something like that," Uncle Jake grunts. "Think of it as a war, Tyler. Long periods of boredom broken up by brief moments of complete mayhem."

92

3 A.M. Still dusk. Where's the bear? When will the next brief moment of complete mayhem come? It's dead silent outside and inside. Uncle Jake's dozing. I'm thinking back to what's happened these past few days. Duke talking about the rogue bear they were having problems with. That bear eating my M&M's and bread-and-jam sandwiches.

The same bear?

It's a safe bet.

Duke said they're animals with a fantastic sense of smell.

So the bear smelled the ham I burned. He came across the river following the scent. Then maybe he even picked up the scent of humans, and that reminded him of the M&M's and bread-and-jam sandwiches. He was hungry. He found the cabin. It smelled good.

And now we're in the mess we're in.

Sounds like my fault.

Across the room, Uncle Jake grimaces in his sleep and wakes up.

"Oh, Mother," he groans.

"Can I do something?" I ask.

"Distract me," he answers.

Huh? Does he want me to do a song and dance? Perhaps demonstrate my amazing ability to hang a spoon from the tip of my nose?

"How come you don't have a gun?" I ask.

"I despise guns," Uncle Jake answers. "They're nasty, ugly devices of destruction. I've hated them ever since Nam. Every time I hear about another kid bringing one into a school, I curse the man who invented gunpowder."

"Hey, I feel the same way," I agree. "But don't you need one to hunt for food?"

Uncle Jake shakes his head. "I'm not partial to killing wild creatures for food. Don't really see the need for it. I mean, I know we're pretty isolated here on the river, but Anchorage is a two-hour flight away, so I can have most of my provisions flown in. Besides, I built this cabin with grizzlies in mind. I'm not particularly concerned about this one getting in here."

Well, I'm glad he isn't.

Wish I could say the same for myself.

The minutes pass in silence. What are we waiting for? The next attack? Is this freaking me out? *To tell you the truth, YES!*

Across the room Uncle Jake is starting to nod off. I'm feeling pretty drowsy myself.

We've covered up all the windows, so I guess normally I wouldn't be able to see what's going on outside. But there are spaces between the logs around the window that the bear damaged, and through the spaces I catch the red glint of the morning sun. It's so strange how you go from day to dusk to dawn without ever seeing the night.

My eyelids are heavy. I guess it won't hurt to take a little nap. In the morning, or whenever I wake up, I'll get in the skiff and head back over to the other shore. I'll grab my fly rod quickly, and then never go near that side of the river again. . . .

Screeeechhhhh! A horribly loud scraping sound jolts me out of my dream state. It's like the sound of fingernails scraping a blackboard. Across the room Uncle Jake's eyes are wide. We hear a loud metallic *clank!* Then the loud squeak of wood being compressed.

Uncle Jake's eyes go upward. "Oh, Mother!" he gasps. "He's on the roof!"

21

The door to Jake's room flies open and Richard bursts out. Above us the ceiling dips under the monster's weight. We all stare up at it.

It's almost comical. Who do we think we are? Supermen with X-ray vision? We can't see through the roof.

Richard grabs the broomstick spear, but how can he possibly stick it through the ceiling?

Creak! The ceiling sags under the bear's weight. We can actually see the boards bend in. Will it give way and collapse? Will the bear crash down to the floor among us?

"We have to get him off the roof," Uncle Jake grunts.

The question is, how?

Clank! Inside the cabin the stovepipe that rises up through the ceiling from the woodstove vibrates. I can only guess that up on the roof the bear took a swing at it.

Clank! The whole stovepipe shakes and rattles.

"What's he doing?" I gasp.

"I doubt he knows," Uncle Jake answers. "But if I were a bear I'd probably do the same thing."

"Why?" I ask.

Clang! Suddenly the whole stovepipe breaks off the stove and swings sideways. Smoke starts to pour out of the top of the stove where the pipe was. The cabin is quickly filling with smoke.

"That's why!" Uncle Jake yells. "Richard, dump some water in there."

"Put out the fire?" Richard frowns.

"Unless you want to choke to death," Uncle Jake warns.

Doris wakes up, blinks, and instantly looks scared. I can't say I blame her. The smoke in the cabin is getting thicker.

Clang! Above us the bear hits the stovepipe again.

Bonk! Inside, the loose end of the pipe swings without warning and smacks Richard in the nose.

"Ow!" Grabbing his nose, Richard reels backward.

"The stove, Tyler!" Uncle Jake shouts at me.

I rush to the sink, quickly pump some water into a pail and then pour it into the stove. A loud *hissssss* and a cloud of steam erupts.

"More water!" Uncle Jake yells.

By now the smoke is twice as thick, and we're all starting to cough. My eyes are burning. I struggle back to the sink and pump more water into the pail, then dump it into the stove.

Hisssssssssss! More smoke and steam erupt from the stove. The smoke's so thick I can hardly see across the cabin. We're all coughing, gasping for breath. My eyes are burning so bad I have to keep them shut. There's no way we can stay in here. The bear can't know it, but he's about to smoke us out!

22

"Down on the floor!" Uncle Jake yells.

Right! That's what books say to do in a fire. Heat and smoke rise, so the cool fresh air will be down on the floor.

Too bad we can't open the windows to let the smoke out!

"Into my room!" Uncle Jake tells us. "Crawl!"

His room? I know why! He wants to use the radio. I crawl on my stomach through the smoke behind Richard, who's helping Doris. The floor is sticky with smeared blood. It must be from Richard's nose.

"Over here!" Uncle Jake grunts in his room. He's crawled to the spot in the floor where Tyler and I pulled up the floorboards. The space be-

Todd Strasser

neath the floorboards is filled with fluffy grayish stuff that looks and feels like big gobs of belly-button lint.

"Dig the insulation out!" Uncle Jake croaks between coughs.

So that's what the stuff is!

I start to scoop it out. Meanwhile Uncle Jake pulls the radio down to the floor and fiddles with the dials.

About eight inches down my knuckles scrape wood.

"I've hit the bottom."

"That's the subfloor!" Uncle Jake wheezes. "Break through it!"

"With what?" I yell back.

"I don't know . . . your foot."

I get up and jam my foot down against the subfloor. *Thunk!* It doesn't give an inch.

"It's too strong!" I cough.

"Keep trying!" Uncle Jake urges me.

Thunk! Thunk! Thunk! It's hopeless! The floor's too strong. Coughing and gasping for breath, I have to drop back down and get some better air.

"I couldn't do it!" I gasp. "It wouldn't give."

Richard pushes himself up. The smoke in the cabin is so thick that when he stands up I can't see past his chest.

Thunk! Thunk! Thunk! He stomps on the floor.

Thunk! Thunk! . . . Crack! That sounded like wood cracking!

But Richard drops down, coughing. Uncle Jake looks at me. I know what he's thinking. It's my turn to get up in the smoke and slam my foot down.

So I do it.

Crack! And again. *Crack!*

I can feel the subfloor giving way. Encouraged, I try again.

Crack! Crack! Crack!

My foot goes through and I drop back down to the floor, coughing. My eyes and lungs feel like they're scorched. But at least there's a small hole in the subfloor now. Fresh, cool air wafts up! The four of us press our faces down into the floor like thirsty animals, only it's the air we're drinking up, not water.

It's not until we've all taken several breaths and coughed our brains out that we're able to think about the bear again. Without a word, we all seem to pause from our thirsty gasps of breath to listen.

We hear nothing except the last hisses and crackles of the dying fire in the woodstove.

Where's Mr. Bear?

Is he gone? Or is he still sitting on the roof?

Uncle Jake immediately turns back to the radio. I can hear some *bleeps* and static coming out of it.

"Darn it!" he grumbles.

"What's wrong?" I ask.

"Bear must've knocked down the antenna," Uncle Jake informs us. "I hate to say this, kids, but it looks like we're going to have to get ourselves out of this alone."

23

We lay around the hole in the floor, just breathing and listening. Everyone has red-rimmed, bloodshot eyes from the smoke.

What now?

What next?

What am I doing here?

Too late to worry about it, Tyler.

"I don't hear anything," I whisper to Uncle Jake. "You think he's gone?"

"I think he's sitting on the roof," my uncle whispers back.

"What do we do?" asks Richard.

For a long moment Uncle Jake doesn't speak. Then he suddenly grimaces. He squeezes his eyes closed and the blood drains from his face.

I don't know exactly what he's feeling, but it must be awful. After a moment the pain seems to pass. My uncle opens his eyes and blinks out some involuntary tears.

"There's only one thing I can think of," he says breathlessly. "And it's awful risky. Trouble is, I don't see any alternatives."

Richard and I share a glance. Neither of us says a word.

"There's an old trapper's cabin about a mile upriver from here," Uncle Jake goes on. "No one uses it anymore, but I used to try to keep it up. Never know when it might save some lost soul's life. I sort of remember some torches in there. Some trapper had 'em on poles and burned them when the mosquitoes got bad. That's what we need right now."

"This bear's a lot bigger than a mosquito," I point out.

"Bears don't like fire," Uncle Jake replies. "If we can get those torches, maybe we can keep that bear away long enough to get to the skiff."

"Maybe?" I repeat.

"Nature doesn't come with guarantees," Uncle Jake chuckles sourly. "And neither do bears."

"And what happens when we get to the skiff?" I ask.

"About five miles upriver is a small village

called Rawson Hot Springs. They'll be able to call for help."

"So, someone has to go to the trapper's cabin and get the torches," I surmise.

"That's correct," answers Uncle Jake.

"But how?" I ask. "It's not like one of us can walk out the front door."

Uncle Jake points down into the hole in the floor. "There's a foot of crawl space under the cabin," he explains. "It's not much, but it's enough to slip through and get out."

"Won't the bear notice?" I ask.

"Not if we distract him," Uncle Jake answers.

24

I can't say I'm disappointed when Uncle Jake chooses Richard to go. He's the logical choice because he knows the woods and this is his home turf. On the other hand, I'm a total stranger here.

By now a lot of the smoke has seeped out of the cabin, which makes it easier for us to breathe. Richard goes back into the main cabin room and gets the tools. We're going to have to make the hole in the subfloor larger so he can crawl out.

It doesn't take long to saw a larger hole. But the sound of the saw seems to annoy the bear, who lumbers around on the roof above us. It's easy to track his movements. Wherever he goes, the ceiling creaks and sags frighteningly. While Uncle Jake never says anything, I definitely get the feeling he's worried that the roof may give way, dropping a hungry, murderous bear into our midst. In that case, the cabin will no longer be our protection. Instead, it will be a cage from which none of us will escape.

Finally the hole in the floor is big enough for Richard to slip through.

"Here's the plan," Uncle Jake explains. "We distract the bear and Richard crawls out."

"How?" I ask.

"We'll have to uncover the window and throw out something that he'll like," my uncle says.

"But won't that sort of confirm to the bear that we've got food he wants?" I ask.

Uncle Jake lets out a long sigh as if he hadn't thought of that, then nods slowly. "Yes, Tyler, it will. But I have a feeling he knows that anyway. And I just don't see what other choice we have. If we don't do something, who knows how long that bear will stick around? And even if he leaves for a while, he could come back at any time. It's not like he's going to forget that he smelled something delicious around here. That creature's a rogue now, and we won't be safe until either he or we are gone."

Okay, I can accept that. It's not like any of us really knows. "One more question?" I ask.

"Let's hear it," says Uncle Jake.

"I understand the part about distracting the bear long enough for Richard to get away. But what happens when Richard tries to come back?"

Uncle Jake blinks and rubs his chin. He gives Richard a questioning look and then turns back to me. "I hate to say it, Tyler, but that's a darn good question. I guess we'll have to distract the bear a second time."

"But how will we know when to do it?" I ask.

Uncle Jake thinks quietly, then says, "Richard, know any animal calls?"

Now it's Richard's turn to think for a moment. He cups his hands over his mouth and makes a soft *"Woooooo-hoooooo"* sound.

Uncle Jake frowns. "What the heck's that?"

"Arctic loon," Richard answers.

"Never heard of it," says Uncle Jake.

"It is not around here," Richard explains. "From back home. Around Norton Sound."

"Well, okay," Uncle Jake says. "We'll listen for that. If we're lucky, when the bear hears it, he'll be just as confused as I was."

Richard nods grimly. It's obvious that he's not keen about going on this adventure.

Who could blame him?

The next step is to go into the main cabin room and as quietly as possible start to pry the barricade off one of the windows. Uncle Jake wants me to throw some food in one direction while Richard crawls off in the other direction. The idea being that Richard'll beat it into the woods while the bear is busy chowing down on whatever I throw out to it.

Richard and I get most of the wood off the window, but Uncle Jake wants me to leave the final piece on until the last moment. He figures I'll be able to distract the bear first with the noise and then with the food.

Once again, we gather around the hole in the floor.

Uncle Jake gives Richard a stern look. "Ready?"

Richard nods.

"You're safe under the cabin," Uncle Jake says. "Crawl to the edge, then knock on the floor three times when you're ready to run. I'll tell you when to go."

Richard leans over the hole and sticks his head in.

Suddenly Doris starts to whimper.

"It's okay, Doris." Uncle Jake tries to reassure her while Richard slithers a little farther into the hole.

But Doris just whimpers more loudly and grabs on to her brother's leg. Richard backs out of the hole and speaks to her in a low, harsh voice. It's his native language, and I don't understand a word. Just the same I know he must be warning her to leave him alone and let him go.

No matter what Richard says, Doris keeps shaking her head. Now she starts to cry. This is really pitiful. The kid is really scared. Richard barks angrily at her one more time and again ducks into the hole. But as soon as he does, Doris wraps her arms around his leg. Talk about bear hugs. She's not going to let him go anywhere.

And we all know it.

Once again Richard looks out of the hole. While he glares angrily at his sister, Uncle Jake gives me a questioning look.

It takes me a second to realize what he's thinking.

Oh, no! He can't be serious!

25

Uncle Jake is serious.

"I'd do it if I could, Tyler," he says quietly. "But there's no way I'll make it in this pain. And I can't make you do it, either. Lord knows your mother would have my head if she knew. But frankly, given a choice between your mother taking my head and that bear eating it, I'd have to go with your mother."

So it's up to me. Uncle Jake gives me the instructions on how to find the trapper's cabin and what to do when I get there. Richard even gives me a quick lesson on the call of the arctic loon.

How's this for a hoot? Outside there's a bear sitting on the roof waiting to eat us. Inside Richard and I are sitting on the floor with our hands cupped around our mouths, going *"Woooooo-hoooooo."*

But it's not a hoot for long because I can tell by the look on my uncle's face that he wants me to go. I look down through the hole in the floor. It looks dark and the air smells earthy and moist. Uncle Jake gives me one last nod. Then I duck my head down and start to crawl.

The earth under the cabin is soft and moist, but surprisingly cold. I remember reading something about permafrost—this layer of frozen earth below the surface that in some places never thaws. It wouldn't surprise me if eight inches below this soft, damp soil is a layer that is frozen as hard as rock.

I crawl under the cabin until I reach the edge. The light is dull outside, and the air feels cool and damp. I have a feeling it's gotten cloudy. I don't know whether that's a good sign or not.

I rap my knuckles three times on the floor to let Uncle Jake know I'm ready to run. A few moments later I hear a faint creaking sound, which must be Richard taking the last piece of wood off the window.

Everything is still for a moment.

Then the whole cabin trembles and shakes. It can only mean one thing—the bear is climbing down to go after the bait.

Behind me I hear rustling as Uncle Jake sticks his head into the hole in the floor. "Go, Tyler!" he hisses.

26

I crawl out from under the cabin and run as fast as I can to the edge of the clearing and then plunge into the woods. Uncle Jake said I would see a trail. Well, I don't, and frankly, I'm not about to take the time to stop and look for it. Not with that bear somewhere behind me. I've just got to have faith that I'll come across it soon.

I keep thrashing through the undergrowth, climbing over fallen tree trunks and around rocks. There's only one thing I care about, and that's getting away and not hearing the sound of that huge bear crashing through the woods behind me. As I run, I study the trees ahead of me, looking for the ones with lots of branches to climb in case the bear comes. Uncle Jake warned me that if I hear the bear coming, I'll have to climb fast and high. He said grizzlies don't usually climb trees, but standing on their tiptoes they can still reach pretty high up.

The woods seem endless, directionless. Where's the trail Uncle Jake said I'd see? After a while I have to stop and catch my breath. Between gasps I listen for the sound of a rampaging bear. But the forest is silent. It looks as if Uncle Jake's plan has worked.

So far.

I look around again for the trail. The forest floor of pine needles and moss is soft underfoot. Looking up I get only an occasional glimpse of the sky through the tops of the spruces, but it's enough to tell me that it's gray and cloudy. It feels as if it's growing darker. I can feel the weather changing. The air is growing cooler and more moist.

Great. Here I am alone in the Alaskan woods, and a storm is blowing in!

I better find that cabin. But to do it, I need to find the trail. So where is it? I look around and see nothing but tree trunks.

It's starting to drizzle. I don't like this. Stay calm. Don't panic. Uncle Jake said the cabin was right along the river.

So where's the river? Where am I?

I don't know, but I'd better keep going.

I start walking again. I hope I'm walking toward the river, but how would I know?

Minutes pass. I know time stretches out in situations like this, but it still feels as if I should've gotten to the river by now. Why didn't I join the Boy Scouts? I bet I would've learned all kinds of tricks, like how to weave an emergency raincoat out of pine needles and make a compass out of mosquito wings.

It's started to rain, but I'm pretty dry under the trees. Too bad the trees can't tell me which way to go. In this unexpectedly cool weather I suddenly realize I'm shivering. Maybe I should stop and go in another direction.

But I keep walking. Half my brain says *Stop! this is stupid, you're just wasting energy*. The other half of my brain says *Keep going! the river could be right around the next tree*. I keep telling myself I know where I'm going. The alternative is too scary to think about.

It's starting to rain harder. The trees aren't offering much protection, and I'm starting to get wet.

I'm walking in a cloud of fear. There's been no sign of any trail. There's nothing but trees in every direction. *You're lost, Tyler!* It began as a little whisper, but now it's a huge roar in my ears. Here I am, in the middle of a state three times the size of Texas, with something like one fiftieth the population. I don't know where I am, or where I'm going. I can't see more than fifty feet in front of me. Uncle Jake and Richard and Doris are back there somewhere with a huge bear waiting to eat them. My teeth are chattering, and my arms and back are covered with goose bumps. Is it from the cold or the fear? Maybe both.

Whoa!

The ground disappears beneath me and I start to fall. The next thing I know, I'm sliding down over rain-slicked rocks that line a small ravine, maybe twelve or fifteen feet deep. I'm banging and thumping into hard edges. I grab at the cold wet rock, but it just slides under my fingers.

I hit the bottom of the ravine and just sit there. I mean, I've hit bottom in more ways than one. I'm lost and alone. My ribs sting from being scraped on the rocks. The raindrops bead up on my face. What's the point of getting up? What's the point of doing anything? I'm a freezing twelve-year-old kid lost in the middle of Alaska. I'm gonna die.

27

The thoughts that go through my mind are weird. I guess it takes a moment like this for you to understand how much you don't belong in a place. Human beings aren't wilderness animals. They don't have fur to keep them warm or claws to hunt with. It may be easy to *imagine* yourself backpacking into the wilderness with your sleeping bag and tent and fishing rod, but the reality is something totally different. It's *hard* to be out here. It's hard to survive when you're defenseless and soft and you're no longer on the top rung of the food chain.

But thinking like this isn't helping. *Do something, Tyler.* Anything is better than sitting on the bottom of this dried-up stream bed. Overhead the gray clouds race by with typical Alaskan speed. *Don't give up. Don't wait for someone to tell you what to do, because there's no one here.* But I don't know what to do.

Under my shirt rainwater runs off my shoulders and down my arms, and I feel a chill. Got to get out of this rain before I catch pneumonia. It would be nice if I could find the cabin, too.

"Think," I say aloud to myself.

Find the cabin.

To do that I need to find the river.

To do that I have to figure out where I am.

But I don't know where I am. I'm lost in a forest. I'm lost, I'm scared, I'm gonna . . . Stop, don't freak out. Think . . . *Think!* The sun rises in the east and sets in the west. But up here the sun doesn't set. It just sort of goes around in a circle, and anyway it's behind the clouds. Which way is the wind blowing? Can you tell the direction from the trees? I look up and see the clouds going past. East to west? West to east? What would it mean anyway? I don't know.

Even without moving, fear makes my heart race in my chest. Don't freak out. Stay calm. There has to be a way out. Think of all those pioneers who wandered through wilderness North America. How did they know where to go? Maybe they didn't. Maybe they just knew how to survive wherever they went. If there's one thing you don't learn in San Francisco, it's how to survive in the woods.

If I concentrate maybe I can figure it out. Look at the trees, the sky . . . The rain's coming down. Water goes down. *Wait! That's it! You crazy nut! It's so simple!* Water goes down and becomes little rivulets on the ground. Little rivulets become brooks. Brooks feed into creeks. Creeks feed into little rivers. Little rivers feed into big rivers. I'm sitting in a creek bed. I quickly turn around and look behind me. The creek bed is definitely sloping down toward me. In front of me it slopes away. If I follow this brook, I should come to a river. I never heard Uncle Jake talk about any other river around here besides the Kantishna. I get up and start running over the rocks. This has got to be it. It just has to be.

At the first glimpse of the broad gray-green river ahead I feel like Moses entering the promised land. I can't have gone more than a quarter of a mile, but if I hadn't stumbled into that creek, I'd still be lost in the forest.

Minutes later I kneel on all fours like a wild animal by the edge of the Kantishna. My clothes are soaked from the rain and I'm freezing. But suddenly I feel incredibly thirsty. All I want to do is dip my hands in the water and drink.

The ice-cold water tastes good. One more drink and I better head upstream and look for that trapper's cabin.

I make my way along the shoreline. A large fish leaps and splashes out in the river. I wonder if he's thumbing his nose at me. Like, *"You came to Alaska to eat me, and instead you're the one who's going to get eaten!"*

It's so weird. I mean, who could have imagined?

I walk upstream just like Uncle Jake said I should. The trees are mostly tall spruces and short black pines.

What if I miss the cabin? What if it's empty, abandoned, burned to the ground? My life depends on that cabin. Uncle Jake's and Richard's and Doris's lives depend on me. The insane thing is it's not a video game. It's real. I have to keep winning, because when the quarter runs out, it isn't just the game that's over. So is someone's life.

It's a miracle when the cabin pops into view. Just like Uncle Jake said, it's up on stilts at the back of a small clearing facing the Kantishna, surrounded by a grove of huge, ancient white pine trees. The cabin is old, the wood is dark gray and weather-beaten.

As I make my way through the tall grass, the feeling of triumph starts to disappear. From the outside I can see that the cabin's a wreck.

The single window is smashed and the front door dangles loosely by one hinge. I climb a rickety ladder made of odd planks hammered to a couple of long poles, and swing the door back.

The inside of the cabin has to be one of the strangest things I've ever seen. It's almost completely lined with old tarnished aluminum foil. It looks like one of those old-fashioned renderings of a house in space. Like something out of Jules Verne or H. G. Wells. I guess the foil must have something to do with keeping the heat in. My more immediate concern is that it looks like a hurricane hit it. More likely, a bear. A few dented cans lying on the floor have serious gashes in them, and there are deep claw marks on the cabinet as well.

But at least it's dry.

The cabin is a single square room, a box. I doubt anyone, or anything larger than a raccoon, has been inside in years. A layer of dust covers the floors, thick spiderwebs span the corners. Near the entrance is a small counter and a metal sink with a stopper but no faucets. In the middle of the room is a small iron stove with a pipe chimney poking up through the roof. There's a chair, a shelf with some books, and a couple of candleholders. Against the wall are about twenty rusty iron animal traps of various sizes.

And there in the corner are the torches.

28

I gather up the torches and climb down out of the trapper's cabin. There's no time to lose. I have to head back. Hey, wait a minute! If I didn't take the trail here, how am I going to find my way back? The answer is the riverbank. I'll follow it until I come to the inlet where Uncle Jake keeps the skiff.

It actually works. Twenty minutes later I'm in the woods surrounding the cabin. But where's the bear? Is he around the cabin? Is he in the woods with me? Carrying the torches, I walk quietly, constantly looking around. I always have a tree in mind to sprint to should the bear suddenly appear.

I manage to circle the cabin. I can just barely

make it out through the tree trunks. Amazingly, the bear is sitting on the roof again. Like a king on his throne. Just sitting there licking his paw and passing the time of day.

I cup my hands around my mouth and do my best arctic loon imitation. *"Whooooooo-hooooooo!"*

The bear's ears instantly perk up, and he stops licking his paw. He pokes his nose up in the air and sniffs like a dog.

Come on, guys, throw the bait! What are you waiting for?

But the bear hasn't budged from the roof. Something's not right. Maybe they didn't hear me. I cup my hands around my mouth again. *"Whooooooo-hooooooo!"*

The bear swings his head in my direction. In a flash he's up on all fours on the roof. The hair on his back is standing straight up, and he's gnashing his teeth. Why do I have the feeling my arctic loon imitation didn't fool him?

Oh, no! He's on the move, across the cabin roof. And he's not exactly lumbering. He's moving fast. He jumps down and hits the ground with a *thud!* I don't have time to see what he does next. I'm too busy dropping the torches and heading for the nearest tree.

I reach the tree and start to climb. The smell of pine sap is in my nose. I can feel its stickiness on my hands as I haul myself up through the branches. But what I'm most aware of is the sound of the bear crashing through the underbrush toward me. Uncle Jake said you had to get at least twelve feet off the ground.

Right now I can't be more than six feet up.

I look down.

He's right under me!

29

The tree shakes as the bear crashes up through the lower branches. I hear a loud *Rippp!* and feel a burning sensation across the back of my leg. With one last burst of energy I scramble the rest of the way up and out of reach.

Phew! I know he got me, but at least I'm alive. The back of my leg burns, but at the same time it feels like nothing more than a real deep scratch.

Now I hear someone yell from the cabin. On the ground below me the bear hears it, too. His ears prick up and he turns around. *Clang! Clang!* In an effort to attract the bear's attention, they must be banging metal pots and plates together.

The next thing I know, the bear takes off back toward the cabin. Oh, great! That means I'm probably supposed to climb back down. No rest for the weary, I guess. Luckily my wound isn't bad enough to hurt my mobility, and I quickly climb down, grab the torches, and run toward the cabin like a madman. Ahead I can see the bear in the clearing, eating something Richard must've thrown out for him. I get to the edge of the cabin and quickly crawl into the shadow underneath, out of the bear's reach. *Phew!* I can't ever remember being this happy to crawl on my stomach in cold dirt.

Ahead of me, Richard sticks his head through the hole in the floor and stares at me upside down. He gives me a grim look. Gee, you'd think he'd be glad to see me with these torches.

I crawl over to the hole in the floor and shove the torches through. Then I crawl through myself.

Once I'm back inside the cabin, I see why Richard looks so grim. Uncle Jake is curled up in fetal position on the floor. His eyes are squeezed shut. He must be in terrible pain.

"I know he looks bad," I tell Richard. "But we've got the torches now. At least we can try to get out of here."

Richard nods in agreement. "But Jake cannot walk."

30

"If he can't walk, how are we going to get him out of here?" I ask.

Richard bites his lip and looks around. He stops and stares at the door. No, it's as if he's looking *through* the door.

"The wagon," he says.

Of course! The wagon we carried the supplies in!

Looks as if we're going to load and unload it one more time.

We help Uncle Jake to the door. It's not easy. He's in a lot of pain and moans and winces with every step.

Next, Richard opens the big can of kerosene and dunks in the torches. P.U.! In no time the whole cabin reeks of kerosene fumes. At this point we have to get out of here just to get away from the fumes. Doris is carrying a day pack with emergency provisions for our trip.

The next step in the plan is to throw food out the window to distract the bear while we make our getaway. We can see that he's just about finished the last treat Richard threw him. I figure the more the better, so I throw the ham and just about everything else I can find.

But the ham must be the prize the bear was waiting for, because he picks it up in his jaws and lumbers into the woods.

I sure hope he plans to take his time eating it, because the kerosene fumes are killing us. Like it or not, we've got to go!

We push open the door and head out. With each of us supporting one of Jake's arms, Richard and I move my uncle across the porch and down the steps. Then Richard sprints across the clearing and comes back with the wagon.

"What the . . . ?" Uncle Jake frowns, then actually smiles a little once we start to help him into the wagon. "Now, *this* is the way to travel!"

We get him into the wagon and then put a blanket over him. Holding a burning torch in one hand, Richard pulls the wagon. I push from behind with one hand while holding another burning torch. Doris walks just beside the wagon so we can keep an eye on her.

There's no sign of the bear. So far . . .

It's not easy to push the wagon with one hand, and it's slow going. My heart is beating like mad. Richard and I are like the President's secret service men, constantly looking around for danger as we slowly go down the trail toward the inlet where the skiff lies.

Somehow we make it all the way down the trail to the skiff. It's like some kind of miracle!

We waste no time getting Uncle Jake into the skiff and helping him lie down on the floor. Next we get Doris into the bow.

Finally everything's ready. We ditch the torches in the water. Richard gets in and pulls on the engine cord to start the boat, and I shove off.

A few moments later we're motoring out toward the middle of the river. It's pretty slow going against the current with the four of us aboard, but at least we're on the water!

It truly seems like a miracle.

Until Doris screams.

31

It's the bear!

He's swimming toward us across the current!

His nose, eyes, and ears stick out of the water, and he's snorting and coughing as if he's half choking on water as he swims.

I guess that ham just wasn't enough. . . .

With the skiff weighed down by the four of us we're not making enough progress against the current. The bear is coming across the river. At this rate he's going to catch us.

"Turn around!" I shout at Richard.

He frowns as if he can't understand why.

"If we go with the current, we'll go faster!" I shout.

"But that's away from Rawson Hot Springs!" he shouts back.

I point at the bear. "Yeah, but at this rate we're never gonna get there anyway!"

Richard gets the idea and swings the boat around.

Thunk! Clank! The skiff suddenly shudders. We've hit a rock! We were so busy watching the bear, we weren't paying attention. The little outboard engine roars uncontrollably. I know what that means. The prop's broken and spinning free. We've just lost power.

The bear's only fifty feet away now. He's made it out of the deep part of the river. His head and shoulders come up out of the water as his feet touch the river bottom.

Luckily for us the gravel bar Duke used as a runway is on the other side of the boat.

"Come on!" I shout, jumping out of the boat and into the cold water. Richard jumps out, too, and together we drag the boat through the icy shallows and up onto the gravel bar.

We quickly get Doris out of the skiff. She hurries toward the far end of the gravel bar. But what about Uncle Jake? Should we try to get him out of the skiff?

Meanwhile, the bear is splashing into the shallows approaching the bar. The water's only up to his belly now, and he's moving faster. We wouldn't have time to get Uncle Jake out of the skiff even if we wanted to.

"Some people say you should wave your arms and shout your lungs off at it. Sometimes the bear will stop and reconsider."

"Go away!" I yell, waving my arms. "Scoot! Vamoose! Get lost!"

Richard frowns at me, but then he, too, starts to shout and wave.

Meanwhile, the bear is coming out of the water and toward us.

"Go! Get lost! Go away!" We shout and wave.

The bear's on the gravel bar now. He's not going away. He's gaining speed.

"Go! Stop! Get away!" Richard and I wave as hard as we can and shout as loud as we can.

Not that it's doing any good!

The bear's bearing down on us.

Richard stops shouting and gives me a terrified look.

"Why don't you leave us alone?" I scream.

32

Incredibly, as if it's heard me, the bear skids to a stop on the gravel. Richard and I watch in total amazement as it rises up on its hind legs and perks up its ears.

Encouraged, I scream, *"That's right! Get out of here! Leave us alone!"*

Still on its hind legs, the grizzly squints and turns its head.

"Go! Go! Go!" I shout and wave.

The bear drops back down to all fours and hurries off the gravel bar, splashing back into the water.

"It worked!" I shout triumphantly, swinging my fist in the air. "Did you see that, Richard? It worked!"

"No." Richard shakes his head.

"What do you mean?" I sputter. "You saw what happened. I yelled and waved my arms, and it changed its mind."

Richard keeps shaking his head. "Listen."

I listen. In the distance I can hear the faintest hum. Richard and I look around. A tiny dot is growing against the gray sky. It's a plane.

"They have an incredible sense of hearing," Duke said.

Right. So of course the bear would hear the airplane long before we would. *That's* why it splashed back into the water.

So who cares why it's gone? The good news is it's gone!

Richard and I share a *Whoop!* and a high five and—

"Hey, wait a minute!" I gasp.

"What's wrong?" asks Richard.

"How do we know that plane is headed for us?" I ask.

33

What follows is the old airplane dance with Richard and me jumping around and waving our arms and shouting.

"Know what's weird?" I ask as we do this.

"I know," Richard replies. "Before we were doing this to scare away the bear."

"You got it," I reply.

The good news is that the plane seems to be heading straight toward us. Is it my imagination, or is it also descending as it gets closer?

Soon there's no doubt that it's headed for us. It's Duke and his old blue Cessna! Boy, am I glad to see him!

He passes over us so low I can see his face in the window. He's frowning at the sight of us on

135

the gravel bar and Uncle Jake curled up in the skiff. Of course he can't understand what's going on because the bear's gone back into the river.

Duke circles around for a second pass. He makes gestures with his hands for us to clear out so that he can land.

Once again he circles the gravel bar, then comes in low over the water. With a loud crunching sound the wheels of the Cessna strike the bar and the plane rolls almost from one end of the bar to the other before it stops.

This time Duke manages to stop on the bar itself and not in the water.

The door of the Cessna swings open, and Duke jumps down and starts jogging toward us. The expression on his face says it all. He looks worried sick. You can see how much he cares about Uncle Jake.

"What's wrong?" he asks as he hustles up and kneels down beside the skiff.

"Uncle Jake said it was kidney stones," I tell him.

Duke puts his hand on Uncle Jake's forehead. "How long's he been like this?"

"He's been in pain ever since I got here," I answer. "But it only really got bad today. But you weren't supposed to come back for two weeks. How'd you know we needed you?"

"I didn't," Duke answers. "When I took those

hunters up to the Anaktuvuk yesterday, I real-
ized I still had Jake's mail. I just figured I'd
drop it off on the way back. Tell you what, Tyler.
Run over to the Cessna. There's a first-aid kit
behind the pilot's seat. Maybe we can make your
uncle a little more comfortable before we get
him out of here."

"Right." I jump up and run down the gravel
bar to the Cessna. I pull the pilot's seat forward,
and there's the first-aid kit. I grab it and turn
back to the others.

But then I freeze.

The bear is lumbering back onto the gravel
bar.

34

The bear has come up on the bar between me and the others. He's facing away from me, and even though his fur is dripping wet, some of it still stands straight up on his back. I can hear his teeth grinding.

I can see Richard and Doris staring at the bear.

But Duke is staring past the bear . . . at me. "The shotgun!" he shouts.

I turn back to the Cessna and yank the passenger seat forward. There it is. I grab it and back away from the plane. I've never fired a real gun before. I've never even *held* a real gun before. The first thing you notice is how heavy it is. This thing weighs a ton! All I know is you put the stock against your shoulder, aim, and pull the trigger.

I jam the stock against my shoulder and aim down the barrel.

Wait! The bear is directly between me and the others. If I miss the bear I could hit Duke or Richard or Doris!

"Shoot!" Duke shouts at me.

What am I going to do? If I shoot and hit one of them, I'll never forgive myself.

But if I don't shoot and the bear gets them, I'll never forgive myself, either.

"Go on! Shoot!" Duke screams louder.

I have to do it. I have to take the chance. I pull the trigger.

Nothing happens.

"Shoot, for Pete's sake!" Duke yells.

I squeeze the trigger again.

"I'm trying!" I yell back, squeezing the trigger again. *What's wrong with this stupid thing?*

"I think it's jammed!" I shout.

"The safety!" Duke shouts back.

The safety . . . the safety . . . I stare down at the shotgun. How am I supposed to know what the safety is? There's one other lever on the side of the gun near the trigger. Maybe that's it.

I flick it down and raise the shotgun to my shoulder, aim, and squeeze the trigger.

BLAM!

35

The next thing I know I'm flying backward through the air. I don't know what I expected when I pulled the trigger, but it sure wasn't this. Out of the corner of my eye I see a huge spray of gravel fan up in front of the bear.

Crunk! I hit the ground.

Clatter! The shotgun hits the ground next to me.

I guess this is what they mean by recoil.

Only now when I look up, the picture has changed. The grizzly bear is no longer facing Duke and the others. Now he's facing me!

He starts to charge. I can feel the gravel shaking under me!

"Pump it! Pump it!" Duke is shouting.

140

Pump what? I ask myself as I scramble to my feet.

"The shotgun!" Duke yells as if he's read my mind.

Oh, yeah! I've seen that a million times on TV! I scoop up the shotgun, grab the wooden handle, and slide it back toward me. I hear all sorts of clicks and clacks as a shell ejects. Then I aim.

The bear is barreling toward me like a small brown car.

Every part of my body is shaking. It's almost impossible to aim.

He's only fifty feet away now.

I brace myself and squeeze the trigger.
BLAM!

36

*O*nce again the shotgun kicks, and even though I was ready for it this time, it still knocks me back and swings me around. When I regain my balance and look up, the bear is sitting on the bar forty feet away. His head is down and he seems to be looking at his left shoulder. There's a dark spot there, and although I can't be certain, I have a feeling it may be where I shot him.

"Good shot!" Duke shouts. *"Shoot him again!"*

Again? Why?

The bear's just sitting there. He's not threatening anyone now. I watch as he gingerly licks the spot on his shoulder. You almost have to feel bad for him. Like Uncle Jake said, he's just a big dumb hungry creature looking for a meal.

"Do it!" Duke cries. *"Shoot him!"*

In the deep recesses of my mind I remember something about a wounded animal being even more dangerous than a healthy one. But it still doesn't seem right. The bear's just sitting there. Maybe he'll just give up. If I got shot in the shoulder, *I'd* sure give up.

Uh-oh! The bear's starting to get up again. I think I just discovered one of the major differences between man and bear. He's up on all fours now, grinding his teeth, his hair standing on end.

Maybe I only grazed him.

He charges again.

I aim, knowing this may be the last shot I ever take.

BLAM!

37

This time the bear goes down on his side and lays there on the gravel. He's less than thirty feet away.

I lower the shotgun. This has to be it. It *has* to be over now. There no way . . . Absolutely *no way* he's going to get up.

Meanwhile, at the far end of the gravel bar, Duke and the others watch silently. Even though the bear is down, none of us dares to go near it.

A fine, misty drizzle starts to fall out of the gray sky. My shoulder throbs from the recoil of the shotgun, and the back of my leg still stings where the bear swiped me.

It's dumb to just stand here. We've got to get Uncle Jake into the plane.

We've got to get out of here. . . .

And then I see something unbelievable.

The bear twitches.

Its ears go up.

Then its head rises.

It looks around as if it just woke up from a nap.

I watch in total disbelief as it struggles to its feet. Bright red blood is dripping down the left side of its face.

This can't be happening.

Or if it is, then the bear knows it's time to give up and go away.

But to my total astonishment, it starts toward me. Staggering, snorting.

INVASION OF THE INDESTRUCTIBLE KILLER GRIZZLIES.

But wait! I was only kidding!

The bear's still stumbling toward me.

What in the world can it be thinking?

But that's just it, isn't it? It *isn't* thinking. It's just being a bear.

"*Shoot it!*" Duke's shout rings in my ear.

I raise the shotgun to my shoulder and sight down the barrel.

The bear's only twenty feet away now. I can see its brown eyes and its cute furry little teddy-bear ears.

"*Pump and fire!*" Duke shouts.

145

I pump the shotgun. An empty shells flies out, and I can hear the next round slide into place.

But I don't pull the trigger. I don't want to kill this creature. Even though it wants to kill me, I see something brave and dignified in it. It isn't evil. It's just doing what thousands of years of life have taught its species to do. It's not its fault that it's staggering toward me. It's my fault. If I and all the people like me had never come here, this bear would probably have lived a long, peaceful life.

I can see that Uncle Jake was right. We came here with our idea of how the world should be. And once we came, nothing could ever be the same again.

"*Shoot it!*" Duke cries again.

The bear is only fifteen feet away now. I can't understand why it's still coming, but then maybe I'm not supposed to be able to understand.

Ten feet away the bear stumbles and goes down on its knees.

"*Do it!*" Duke shouts. "*Put it out of its misery!*"

Yeah, at this point I guess that's the only thing that makes sense.

BLAM!

38

As I lower the shotgun to the gravel bar, I find that I'm shaking even more now than before. Next thing I know, my legs go rubbery and I have to sit down. I can hear the crunch of gravel underfoot as Duke jogs toward me.

Guess he knows I'm not going anywhere fast.

Duke pauses beside me and puts his hand on my shoulder.

"I know it wasn't easy," he says solemnly.

All I can do is nod.

"You did good, Tyler." He pats my shoulder. "Chances are you'll never have to do anything like that again."

He takes the first-aid kit and heads back to my uncle. I just sit there thinking.

147

Darn right I'll never have to do anything like that again. Next time I'm DEFINITELY going to Hawaii.

Duke gives Uncle Jake a shot, and then we get him into the plane. Doris sits in the passenger seat next to Duke while Richard and I huddle in the back with my uncle.

We will leave the bear on the gravel bar. No one is going to mount its head on a wall as a trophy. No one is going to spread its hide out on a floor as a conversation piece. I hope no one will bother it, and with time it will return to the earth.

Duke revs the Cessna's engine. We lumber down the gravel bar and take off. Up in the air the noise and vibration shake Uncle Jake awake. He looks around the inside of the plane.

"Everyone okay?" he asks.

"Believe it or not," I answer. "How about you?"

"Pain's not as bad," Uncle Jake answers. "Duke must've given me something, right?"

"Right." I nod. "Don't worry. Everything's gonna be okay. I bet it won't be long before you're back at the cabin."

Uncle Jake stares at me, then shakes his head slowly. "I'm not coming back, Tyler."

"Why not?"

"Guess I finally figured out that I don't belong

there anymore," he says. "It's time to do something new."

"Maybe you'd like to come down to San Francisco and stay with us for a while," I suggest. "I know Mom would like it."

Richard instantly gives me a worried look.

"Hey, you and Doris can come, too," I tell him. "We've got room. And maybe once we're there, Uncle Jake can become an official foster parent."

"I'll definitely consider it," Uncle Jake says, and closes his eyes.

Meanwhile, Richard studies me.

"What is it?" I ask.

"You think maybe we could go to the dog museum?"

"We can sure give it a try." I answer. "But only if you promise to show me what I'm doing wrong in chess."

Richard thinks and then for the first time smiles. "Sounds good."

AUTHOR'S NOTE

According to history, Balto and his team were one of twenty sled dog teams that helped carry the smallpox serum through frigid blizzard conditions to Nome. Balto's team covered the last 53 miles of the journey and that is what made him famous.

Balto's story turned sad after that. He and the other dogs on his team were sold to a Hollywood movie producer who made a movie about them and then sold them to a carnival.

From there, the dogs were sold to a "dime museum," which charged the curious a dime to see what was inside. According to a newspaper story, the dogs were treated terribly during their stay there.

While visiting Los Angeles one day in 1927, a businessman from Cleveland named George Kimball saw the dogs and decided to save them. Back in Cleveland he led a campaign to raise $2,000 to buy Balto and his team.

Later that year, the dogs arrived in Cleveland, where they lived comfortably at the zoo. Balto died in 1933. His body was mounted and placed in the Cleveland Museum of Natural History, where it can still be viewed today.

ABOUT THE AUTHOR

Todd Strasser has written many award-winning novels for young and teenage readers. Among his best known books are those in the *Help! I'm Trapped In . . .* series. Todd speaks frequently at schools about the craft of writing and conducts writing workshops for young people. He and his wife, children, and Labrador retriever live in a suburb of New York. Todd and his family enjoy boating, hiking, and mountain climbing.